Mother
Finds
a Body

FEMMES FATALES

Femmes Fatales restores to print the best of women's writing in the classic pulp genres of the mid-twentieth century. From hard-boiled noir to taboo lesbian romance, these rediscovered queens of pulp offer subversive perspectives on a turbulent era.

Faith Baldwin
SKYSCRAPER

Vera Caspary
BEDELIA
LAURA

Dorothy B. Hughes
THE BLACKBIRDER
IN A LONELY PLACE

Gypsy Rose Lee
THE G-STRING MURDERS
MOTHER FINDS A BODY

Evelyn Piper
BUNNY LAKE IS MISSING

Olive Higgins Prouty
NOW, VOYAGER

Valerie Taylor
THE GIRLS IN 3-B
STRANGER ON LESBOS

Tereska Torres
WOMEN'S BARRACKS
BY CECILE

Mother Finds a Body

GYPSY ROSE LEE

FOREWORD BY ERIK LEE PREMINGER

THE FEMINIST PRESS
AT THE CITY UNIVERSITY OF NEW YORK
NEW YORK CITY

Published by the Feminist Press
at the City University of New York
The Graduate Center
365 Fifth Avenue, Suite 5406
New York, NY 10016

feministpress.org

First Feminist Press edition

Cover and text design by Drew Stevens
Cover photo by Michael Maynard

Library of Congress Cataloging-in-Publication Data

Lee, Gypsy Rose, 1914-1970.
  Mother finds a body / Gypsy Rose Lee.
    p. cm.
  ISBN 978-1-55861-801-5
  I. Title.
  PS3523.E3324M68 2012
  813'.52--dc23

                    2012004491

FOREWORD

My mother's greatest creation was Gypsy Rose Lee, the persona she first adopted as a stripper at Billy Minsky's Republic Theater in New York City in the 1930s. While her fame was rooted in her career as a stripper in burlesque, it flowered into legend through her writing: two successful mystery novels, *The G-String Murders* and *Mother Finds a Body*; several magazine articles for the *New Yorker*, *American Mercury*, *Flair,* and others; and culminated with her memoir *Gypsy*, which became the landmark film and Broadway musical through which Gypsy Rose Lee lives on today.

The progression seems so natural that it must have been easy, but of course it wasn't. She had no formal education, no informal education either for that matter. She spent her childhood trouping in vaudeville with her sister; they never stayed in one place long enough to attend school. Their mother only hired the occasional tutor when there was an overzealous child welfare inspector lurking backstage. When the inspector left, so did the tutor.

So how did she learn to write? She began by reading. Books were her escape from dirty dressing rooms and dismal theatrical hotels, her escape from feeling like a failure because her sister could sing and dance but she could do neither, her escape from the loneliness that she experienced because she couldn't relate to the other children in the act. She didn't know it at the time, but she was, quite simply, smarter than all of them.

She read any book she could buy or shoplift, which resulted in an eccentric range of topics and authors: *Decameron*, *The Blind Bow Boy*, *Painted Veils*, *Das Capital* and *Droll Stories* to name a few. She read them over and over again. She collected so many books that the bottom fell out of her theatrical trunk. After that, her mother made her give up one book for every one she added. My mother used to say that leaving even a bad book was worse than leaving a good friend.

Gradually she learned to be more selective. The manager of the Seven Arts bookstore in Detroit, George Davis, became her first teacher. My mother describes him as "young and delicately handsome. He walked softly on the toes of his feet and when he took the books from the shelves he handled them gently. His voice was gentle, too, and his eyes were sympathetic and warm." Davis suggested she read Shakespeare's sonnets. The next day, the show's engagement in Detroit was over, and she left town with the family troupe.

Skip ahead eight years. Her fortunes had peaked. She had been the toast of New York while at Minsky's, went on to star in the *Ziegfeld Follies* with Fanny Brice, and signed a seven-year contract with Twentieth Century Fox. Then her fortunes plummeted. Will H. Hays—Hollywood's censorship czar—refused to allow the name Gypsy Rose Lee on America's movie screens. Darryl Zanuck, the head of Fox, fulfilled the minimum terms of her contract by putting her in four mediocre, B-grade pictures using her real name—Louise Hovick—and then let her contract option expire at the end of one year. Throw in a marriage to burnish her image for the studio, followed by a divorce as soon as her option was dropped, and she returned to New York demoralized and broke. Stripping was no longer a possibility since Mayor LaGuardia had closed all the burlesque theaters.

Re-enter George Davis. During the same eight years, his fortunes, too, had ebbed and flowed. He had written a wildly successful first novel, but squandered the advance for his second novel on a year's debauch in Paris. He got off the boat with only the clothes on his back, one shoe . . . and the idea to add serious fiction to women's magazines. He created a job for himself as the fiction editor of *Harper's Bazaar,* and introduced to American readers some of the finest writers of the age, among them Carson McCullers, Christopher Isherwood, and Stephen Spender.

George rented a beautiful house in Brooklyn Heights, which he couldn't afford, so he took in boarders to share the rent. At one time or another, his housemates included the poet W.H. Auden; the composer Benjamin Britten; the writers Carson McCullers, Paul Bowles, and Gypsy Rose Lee, and a trained chimpanzee. Everyone was under thirty-five and touched by genius. Inspired by all this talent, Mother began her first mystery.

Her writing was interrupted by the dynamic Broadway showman Mike Todd. He wanted my mother to headline a star-studded review at the New York World's Fair, and she resumed her most lucrative vocation—stripping. A girl's got to make a living you know. Between shows, she wrote in her dressing room, and eventually *The G-String Murders* was published on December 7, 1941. It was not an auspicious debut. The publisher took out full-page ads in newspapers around the country, but that day no one got past the front-page story: Pearl Harbor.

The G-String Murders made the *New York Times* best-seller list, a rare accomplishment at the time. As soon as it did, its authorship was questioned. How could a stripper write such an entertaining, witty book—a best seller no less? Then Mother and George Davis had a falling out over an antique mantle. Mother took the mantle, so he took credit for her book. At the same time, a rumor circulated that mystery writer Craig Rice was the author, a rumor that survives to this day despite the fact that Rice denied it at the time. Mother was furious and frustrated. How does one disprove a negative? She did it by writing another book.

She was the central character in *The G-String Murders*. It was set in a burlesque theater reminiscent of Minsky's, and the characters were thinly veiled representations of the strippers and comics she had worked with. She would also be the central character in her next mystery, *Mother Finds a Body*, and it would also draw on her own experience. The novel is set in a trailer park during her honeymoon—my mother did honeymoon in a trailer—and is populated with burlesque comics, vaudeville actors, and her own mother, whose behavior in the novel was authentic. This novel was not quite as successful so no one else claimed credit for writing it, but her mother did sue her over the book. What's fascinating is that she didn't object to the way she was portrayed; she simply felt she was owed money for acting, so to speak, in the book.

So you may wonder, what was my grandmother really like? My mother said she was "charming, courageous, resourceful, and ambitious. She was also, in a feminine way, ruthless . . . A jungle mother." During interviews I conducted for my memoir, *My G-String Mother*, I was told repeatedly that my grandmother had killed two people: a hotel manager who "fell" out of a window during an argument with her (Arthur Laurents used this as the basis for a scene in the musical *Gypsy*), and her lesbian lover whom she allegedly shot after the woman made a pass at my mother. This was arranged to look like a suicide.

I only met my grandmother a few times; the most time I spent with her was when I was five. It was my job to answer the front door of the twenty-eight-room New York City townhouse where my mother and I lived. One day I opened it to a small, plain woman with curly hair. She asked to see my mother.

"Who shall I say is calling?" I asked. Mother had trained me to be very polite.

"Tell her it's her mother," she answered.

Now my instructions were very clear. I wasn't to let anyone into the house who I didn't know. But this was my mother's mother, and given the high regard in which I held my own mother . . . Well, I invited her to have a seat in the foyer, and then I ran up the three flights of stairs to my mother's room and told her who was waiting.

"Oh, no," my mother said. She waved her hand as if swatting away a fly. "I can't be bothered. Tell her I'm busy." Then, as an afterthought, she asked, "You didn't let her in the house, did you?"

"Well, yes," I admitted.

"Well for God's sake, get back downstairs and make sure she hasn't clipped the Picasso."

I ran back downstairs, checked that the Picasso was in place, and politely told her that my mother was "occupied and couldn't see her."

"Oh, that's all right. I didn't think she'd see me," she said sadly. Then her whole demeanor lightened and she said, "You must be Erik. Come, sit and talk with me for awhile."

So we had one of those long adult/child chats about school and pets, which ended with her saying, "I bet you like guns."

"You bet," I said. Hopalong Cassidy and The Lone Ranger were the heroes of my childhood, and I played with toy pistols galore.

She reached into her purse. "I was cleaning out my attic the other day and ran across this. I thought you'd like to have it."

She pulled out a real .45 caliber army automatic and handed it to me. It was very heavy, and I could hardly lift it, but I was very excited and couldn't wait to play with it, so it came as a disappointment when I showed it to my mother who promptly confiscated it.

Many people have wondered: How much of *Mother Finds a Body* is true? Ultimately, all of mother's writing was based on her life, so by the time she got to *Gypsy* she was comfortable with the characters. Ironically, she waited until after her mother died to write it because she wanted to avoid another lawsuit, but she got sued anyway. This time by her sister. Like the earlier suit by her mother, it was settled with money. To call our family mercenary would be an understatement.

My mother was fifty-nine years old when she died. She claimed to have no regrets; however, throughout her illness she kept saying that as soon as she was better she was going to write another book. We will never get to read that one, so we'll have to make do with the three we have, and consider ourselves lucky at that.

Erik Lee Preminger
2012

1 A TEMPERATURE OF ONE HUNDRED AND TEN, AT night, isn't exactly the climate for asthma or murder, and Mother was suffering from a chronic case of both. She pushed the damp, tight curls off her forehead and tapped her foot impatiently on the trailer doorstep.

"You either bury that body in the woods tonight, or you finish your honeymoon without your mother."

She meant it, too. I could tell from the way she fanned herself with the folded newspaper I'd been saving for my scrapbook. It wasn't a breeze she was after; a hurricane would be more like it. As the paper waved back and forth I could see the caption: GYPSY ROSE LEE WEDS EX-BURLESQUE COMIC IN WATER TAXI. Below, it read: *Biff Brannigan, hit star from* Rings on Her Fingers, *and bride plan honeymoon in trailer.*

The date line was a week old, August 13, Friday, to make it good. That has been my idea; it sounded romantic. The water taxi was my idea, too. I had romance mixed up with tradition on the last thought, but, as it turned out, it had been romantic. The water taxi was like an overfed gondola. A canvas stretched over the front half of it and wooden seats extended front to back. The captain was one we found in a waterfront saloon, and our best man we picked up on the way to the wharf. The Bible came from and all-night mission that served coffee and doughnuts with religion.

11

Even Biff was admitting that it was a wonderful way to get married, when the motor started up and we chugged out to sea. We sat in the back of the boat and I let my hand drag in the cool water. The moon was full and yellow.

"It's like a prop, ain't it?" Biff asked. His voice was low. I think he was awed. "Sort of a Minsky moon. I almost expect the tenor to start singing, 'I'm in love with the daughter of the man in the moon.'"

"Yes," I agreed tremulously. "Then the curtain pulls away and the chorus girls are posing in the sixteen-foot parallels in rhinestone G-strings. The one in the middle holds a flitter star."

One of the longshoremen up front was singing. I couldn't catch all the words, but the song was about a lubber who ought to have his gizzard skewered.

It had been very romantic. But that was a week ago, before we landed in Ysleta, Texas, and found ourselves a corpse. It wasn't a very nice corpse, either. It was quite dead and it had a hole in the back of its head that was big enough for a fist.

"You can't leave a decayed body hanging around in this hot weather," she said. "It's—unhealthy. Asthma or no asthma, I can't stand the odor."

Biff and I had been on friendly terms with corpses before, but even so we didn't refer to them as casually as Mother did. She thought of our latest one as a pound of hamburger or an opened can of beans; we couldn't leave them around in the heat, either.

I had to agree with her about the odor, but I might have pointed out that her newest asthma cure, Life Everlasting, was no bed of heliotrope. As smells go, it ran the corpse a close second.

Mother stopped to wheeze, and Biff used the lull to get in a few words.

"But, Evangie," he said patiently, "when you find a body in your trailer you gotta call the cops. We've been able to stand the odor this long; we can put up with it for one more night and first thing in the morning I'll drive into town and tell the police."

Mother's wheezing ended on a high note. "I'd expect a remark like that from you," she said. "You don't care about my daughter's welfare. You don't care about her career. Go ahead and call the police. Let them drag her name through the newspapers. Let them ruin everything she has worked for all her life!" Mother's voice had reached the hysterical stage and her face was turning red.

Biff recognized the symptoms and rushed into the trailer for the asthma powder. While he was getting it I led Mother to a camp chair under the lean-to tent. As she sat down I tried to reason with her.

"But, Mother, someone sooner or later is going to find out about the corpse. One look and they'll know it's murder. Then they'll find out that he's our best man and . . ."

"How could they find that out?" Mother asked. Her mouth was a thin white line. Her jaw was set firmly. "After all, the man was a total stranger to you. I can't vouch for Biff, but I certainly know you never saw him before in your life."

"Neither did Biff, and you know it. That isn't the point. The idea is we can't touch the body until we notify the police. There's a law about that."

Mother sniffed. "Well, fiddle-faddle such a law. It's inconsiderate."

Biff closed the screen door quietly. He tiptoed over to the table and poured a mound of Mother's asthma powder into a saucer. He touched a match to it. When the flames died down, a sticky-smelling smoke curled up. Mother put a Turkish towel over her head and buried her face in the volcano. Biff and I listened to her labored breathing until it sounded as though the worst part of the attack was over, then I spoke to him.

"Were they sleeping?"

"You mean the dogs, the monkey, the guinea pig, or our guests?" Biff asked. Then he laughed softly. "What a honey-moon! All we need is an olio and we got ourselves a first-class Chautauqua." After a second he answered my question. "Yep, they were sleeping, all right. As usual, they took up the whole damn trailer."

"Well, don't say it as though it's my fault. After all, Mandy and Cliff are your friends. If you want to play Joe Host to every comic on the burlesque circuit, don't blame me when you have no bed to sleep in."

"Gee Gee and Dimples, those two beauties of the runways, are your friends," Biff said pleasantly. Too pleasantly, I thought. "Should I have said no when they asked for a lift?"

"A lift," I said, "is around the corner or up the block, not clear across the country. Furthermore, you don't have to be sarcastic about them. They may not be the beauties you've been working with in *Rings on Her Fingers*, but I'd like to see one of those four-forty legitimate dames do the bumps the way Gee Gee does. Or do Dimples's quiver for that matter."

Biff was on the verge of answering me when we heard the scratching of the screen door. Bill, dachshund, and proud father of four sons, wanted out. His front paws clawed on the wire mesh. He was standing on a white arm. It was Gee Gee's Graham's arm. That was her night to sleep on the floor, and she was sprawled out in front of the door. Her red hair was wet with sweat and she was curled up like a child, with her freckled nose buried in her other arm. When I opened the door for the dog, she gave him a push that sent him rolling down the steps.

"Nice thing," Biff said. "Tossing our watchdog out on his pedigreed rear. Come here, Billy Boy."

Bill waddled over and allowed himself to be petted. Biff rubbed one floppy ear, then the other. The dog whined happily when Biff talked to him.

"He's a busy guy, keeping an eagle eye on his corpse, isn't he? On account of he found it he feels it's sort of personal property, doesn't he?"

Bill wiggled around saying yes.

Mother poked her tousled head out from under the towel. "Please don't forget that *I* found the body," she said. "And as soon as I get over this attack we'll bury it, or I'll take the first train east."

An angry voice from the trailer yelled, "Shut up!" It sounded like Cliff (Corny) Cobb. He was Biff's very good friend and the only comic in burlesque I really disliked.

"If he's got your place in the bed again I'm going to drag him out of it by his big, ugly nose," I said.

I didn't try to keep my voice down; I wanted Cliff to hear me. He had been my pet beef since he joined us in Yuma. And I had my reasons for beefing, too. First of all, he invited himself; moved in, bag and baggage, even after I'd told him how crowded we were. He said he would help Biff with the driving. In the thousand-some miles we had traveled, he hadn't touched the wheel. He was supposed to pay his share of the groceries, too, and so far I hadn't seen the color of his money.

"He's a dead beat, that's what he is."

Biff tried to shush me.

"Oh, shush yourself," I said irritably. "Three weeks now, and he hasn't slept on the floor once. If everyone else can take turns, he certainly can. I told you what it would be like before we left Yuma, but oh, no, you know so much! He's *your* friend. He gets cleaned out in a crap game so he's gotta move in with us. It isn't like he's changed any, either. He was the same selfish, inconsiderate lout when he was on the road with us, too. If there's a good spot in the show, your friend Corny Cobb gets it. He's always grabbing the best makeup shelf, grabbing all your scenes, grabbing everything but a check. No wonder he's the only one who winds up with a buck in the bank at the end of the season. He never paid for anything in his life!"

I must have been screaming, because Mother heard me even though she was still under the towel.

"Gypsy's absolutely right," she said, her voice muffled.

Corny yelled from the trailer again. "Shut up, dammit. Where the hell do you think you are? In a boiler factory?"

I shut up. Not because Corny had requested it in his individual way, but because I had worn myself out. Biff can be so aggravating at times. Instead of putting up an argument when I have one of my fits, he just sits there quietly until I get tired. Nothing infuriates me more and I usually get so mad I want to cry. Instead of crying this time, I started to giggle. The whole picture was suddenly funny to me. A trailer full of people, including one dead one, and me beefing about a comic because he didn't pay his share of the groceries.

Biff wasn't sure that my giggle was his cue. He waited for me to speak.

"We haven't enough to worry about," I said, "I have to make a scene about Corny! I'm sorry, honey."

Biff walked over and kissed me on the nose. He might have done better if the Turkish towel hadn't stirred. Mother could sense emotions even when she was under a towel. After a moment she emerged, red-eyed but businesslike.

"Oh my," she said, "that certainly was a bad one." She folded the towel carefully and placed it on the back of her chair. Then she put out the last of the asthma powder by smothering it with the top of the Life Everlasting container.

"Now we get busy," she said. "You and Louise get a shovel to dig the hole. While you're getting it, I'll go look for a nice burial place." As she walked toward the woods she hummed a little tune: "*I know a place where the sun never shines, where the fou-u-r leaf clovers grow.*"

She stooped over and picked up something. She walked back into the light of the kerosene lamp, examining the pieces of grass she held in her hand.

"See, children," she exclaimed happily, "a four-leaf clover. My little song never misses. That's a sign for you to leave everything to Mother. Everything." Without a backward glance, Mother tucked the four-leaf clover into her curly hair and walked back toward the woods.

"Biff!"she sang out a moment later. "Ask Louise to tell you about the time I found the seventy-one four-leaf clovers."

We both listened to Mother's little song as it became fainter and fainter. Then Biff turned to me. There was something strange in his expression: not exactly fear, but close to it. As though he were puzzled about something that would frighten him if it were true. He waited so long to speak that I became uncomfortable.

"That's true," I said. "About the four-leaf clovers, I mean. She really did find seventy-one of 'em once. On Mother's Day. We were making our jumps by car and, believe it or not, we had five blowouts! While we were waiting for the tow car, Mother started singing her song and before we knew it, there was Mother, with a fistful of clovers."

"Five blowouts doesn't sound very lucky to me," Biff said. He was still staring into the woods. Mother was out of sight, but he kept peering into the darkness.

"In a way it was lucky," I said. "The last blowout was near Akron, Ohio, where they make all those tires. Well, Mother fluffs up her hair and powders her nose and calls on the president of the company. How she gets in to see the head guy is still a mystery, but you know Mother. Anyway, she tells him how we're a travelling vaudeville act and how we have to make Springfield in time for the matinee. Then she cries a little, and ten minutes later, a mechanic comes out and put five brand-new tires on the car! 'No charge,' he tells us. 'The boss is happy to help poor folks out.'"

Biff answered me only because he was trying to be polite. He hadn't been listening very attentively.

"Well, that seems only right to me. Tires are guaranteed," he mumbled.

"Yes, but Mother didn't tell him we'd traveled over fifteen thousand miles on the tires. And I know she didn't mention how they were retreads when we bought 'em."

Biff didn't say anything. Listening to the story again after so many years, I suddenly thought it sounded sort of crooked. I tried to clean it up a little.

"Mother felt that the tire people were rich, and, well, five measly old tires aren't going to break them." My explanation was wasted on Biff.

"Punkin," he said seriously, "I don't like the way Evangie's been acting lately. She's not herself. Oh, I know all the cute little gags about tires for free and swiping other acts' music, but this is different. It's this heartlessness, this coldness, that gets me. I'm a man and I'll be damned if I have nerve enough to bury that body in the dark woods. I should dig a hole and put that corpse in it! The thought of it scares the hell outta me. But look at Evangie! Four-leaf clovers in her hair, humming away like she hasn't got a worry in the world, and out there alone looking for a good burial spot! A good spot, yet, to bury our best man. Do you think maybe the heat's gone to her head or something?"

"Darling," I said slowly, "you knew all about my mother before you married me. You were the one who insisted that as long as she missed our wedding she at least should get in on the honeymoon. You were the one who wired her to join us. Besides, I don't talk like that about your family."

"My family are in the Ramapo mountains," Biff said.

"Don't bring them into it. My mother never wore shoes in her life and my old man never saw a streetcar. They're nice, simple people. They wouldn't know how to cook up schemes like Evangie."

That might have gone on and on, but I heard Mother coming back. She was still humming, and I thought her voice sounded happier than it had for some time. When she neared the trailer I could see her dimly: the pale-blue organdy dress, the half socks to match, the black patent-leather Mary Janes on her feet. Even when she walked into the full light of the lamp, she looked like a little girl. Her cheeks were flushed and she held another four-leaf clover in her hand.

"You know, children, I've just been thinking," she said. Her voice was too calm. I knew something was up. "I've decided that Biff is right. We will wait until morning, then we'll tell the police about the body."

It was too good to be true. I watched Mother closely as she gathered up her toothbrush and towel and things. I watched her as she walked toward the washrooms at the far end of the trailer camp.

"Maybe she means it," Biff said uncertainly.

"Of course she does!" I said. "Are you insinuating that my mother is a liar?"

Biff gulped noisily. Then he began fixing the bed in the back of the automobile. The mattress, the blankets, the pillows—all the things Mother always traveled with were in the trunk of the car. Biff made up the bed and turned on the dome light overhead. He poured out a glass of water and placed it on the small shelf he had built near the headboard for that purpose. Then he put the asthma powder and the matches next to the glass.

"Maybe if we make her real comfy she'll get a good night's rest," he said hopefully.

"Oh, I will." Mother, back from the washroom and scrubbed until she shone like a beacon light, looked fondly at both of us. "How sweet to fix everything so nice," she said. She kissed Biff. Then she kissed me. "Sleep well, darling," she said as she scrambled into her bed.

Biff eyed the folded-up army cot that was his bed, and I peeked into the trailer at the two feet of floor Gee Gee had left me. "We'll sleep like logs," Biff said. In an undertone he added, "And who's kidding?"

2 AT FIVE MINUTES PAST FOUR I WAS STILL TRYING TO get the stove to work. Biff and I had wanted a cup of coffee since we tucked Mother in at midnight. The stove wouldn't draw.

"It's a mechanical difficulty," Biff said for the fifteenth time. He kept poking at the valve with a broom straw.

"It's no fuel, you mean," I said. "I told you to buy a new tube of rock gas before we left San Diego, but oh no, you know everything."

Biff grabbed my arm. "Look!" he said, and pointed.

I thought the red sky was the sun coming up. Suddenly I saw smoke. The camp is near the town dump, as most trailer camps are, and I thought the smoke had something to do with garbage being burned. Then I saw the flames. A second later the entire wood was on fire.

My first thought from then on was for the safety of the animals. I pushed Biff aside as I dashed into the trailer. I don't even remember screaming that the fire was within a few feet of us all. I do remember grabbing up Bill's family, basket and all.

I remember unhooking Rufus Veronica, the monkey, and putting him on my shoulder. Then I scooped up Gee Gee's guinea pig form the bureau drawer and shoved him into my pocket. It wasn't until I tripped over Gee Gee that I had sense enough to arouse our guests.

While I banged on the bedroom door and yelled for Cliff and Mandy to get up, Gee Gee brushed past me, clutching her scrapbook in one arm, her ten-year-old kolinsky scarf in the other.

I rolled Dimples Darling out of bed and threw a kimono at her. She opened her mouth to scream, but Gee Gee pushed her out of the trailer before she had a chance to finish it.

By the time I got out, Cliff and Mandy were leaving by the back door. They were wearing a pair of Biff's pajamas. Mandy wore the bottoms, Cliff the tops. They weren't awake yet and they stared at the flames stupidly.

Dimples screamed then. Not because of the fire, but because of Cliff. She threw him her kimono and rushed back into the trailer. When she came out she had her mangy seat-warped mink coat over her arm. Her hair was rolled up in tin curlers, and she wore a pink rubber chin strap, but for once Dimples Darling wasn't worried about how she looked. She turned the coat inside out and held it close to her chest.

"My last faded rose," she said with a sickly grin. Then she fainted dead away.

By then it seemed the entire trailer camp was up. People in nightgowns and pajamas were running toward the fire with buckets and pails of water in their hands. Someone was thoughtful enough to pour a bucketful on Dimples, and she sat up with a bewildered expression on her wet face.

"W—what's cookin'?" she mumbled.

"You!" Biff snapped, "if you don't get with it." He was searching around for something, and his language was not to be listened to. "Where's that shovel?" is the only part I can translate.

Finally he ran toward a neighbor's trailer and returned in a moment with a large shovel. Then he began digging a trench near our house. As the trailerites passed by, he shouted at them to get shovels and start digging.

"The fire can't jump the trench," he yelled as they stared at him.

It took a full minute for the smartest one to catch on, but when he ran for his shovel, the others followed him blindly.

With that off his mind, Biff started yelling for us to pour water on the trailer so the sparks wouldn't catch. "And get the cars out of the way! The gasoline . . ."

I didn't wait to hear the rest of the direction. With the animals tangled up in my hands and hair, I piled into the driver's seat of our car and drove like mad down the road. When I found a spot that looked safe, I pulled over to the side of the road and turned off the ignition. I tied the monkey to the steering wheel and started to put the dog basket in the back seat. Then I missed Mother! Her bed wasn't mussed; the asthma powder rested on the shelf, the glass of water was spilled over the pillow, but Mother was gone.

I raced back to the trailer camp. Dimples and Gee Gee were pouring bucketfuls of water on our trailer. The dust streaked down the sides in mud streams. Gee Gee was soaking wet, too.

"Where's Mother?" I yelled above the roar of the excited people.

They didn't answer me.

I heard Biff's voice. "Leave our trailer alone," he shouted.

"Get the ones nearest the fire and pour like hell!"

We grabbed the buckets and raced past the safer trailers to those that were in the most danger. The other cars had been driven away, and that meant that the camp was in darkness. Aside from the trailers that carried their own generators, fire was dimmed by the heavy smoke. The wind was blowing toward the end of the camp, and as I ran sparks would catch in the dry grass near my feet, I tried to beat them out with my empty bucket, but they fell so fast!

My eyes burned and I couldn't breathe, but I still kept running toward the fire. It wasn't bravery. I could hear Biff's voice up there and at that moment I would have run through hell to be near him. Whenever the shouting died down for a second I could hear him giving orders. Sometimes he sounded closeby. Then it sounded as though he were miles away. His voice was so calm, so reassuring, that I ran faster.

The handle of the tin bucket was burning my hand. As it hit the side of my leg, I could feel the heat through my heavy slacks. Then suddenly I stumbled into a clearing. The woods weren't woods at all when I saw them close up. The trees were stunted bushes with dried brush piled up around them.

The wind rolled them that way, I thought. But it had been done purposely, it couldn't have made a better bonfire. I saw Biff's shadow coming toward me. Then I heard Dimples.

"To hell with this," she said peevishly. "Here we are, doing all the heavy work. You don't see Corny or Mandy knocking themselves out, do you? Damn right you don't. Well, I don't know about you, but I'm going to get a drink, and fast."

"That's for me," Gee Gee said. "Nothing more we can do, anyway."

One trailer near the woods was still burning. With the sun coming up behind it, it looked like the framework you see in automobile showrooms. A dilapidated car hitched to it was also burning. There was a strong odor of gasoline in the air.

But I hardly noticed anything except that Mother was safe. She was there, talking to a tired-looking woman standing near the burning trailer. The woman was weeping, and I could hear Mother consoling her.

"Such a pity. You didn't even have time to unhitch the car." Mother put her arms around the woman and patted her on the shoulder. "We just got here, too. And to think of driving into all this trouble. But as long as you have insurance, there's nothing to cry about. You can get a new car and trailer. One like my daughter's . . ." Mother saw me and rushed into my arms. "Isn't it the most terrible thing, Louise?" Under her anxious voice I caught a hint of satisfaction.

I felt a tight feeling in my throat. Just like when the manager of a theater would come backstage and ask to talk to me. I could always tell when they were going to ask me questions about Mother. It might be nothing more than a missing letter, a costume flushed down a toilet, or a piece of music missing. I would know then that Mother was "protecting my interests" again.

Sometimes it was worse. Mother loves writing letters. She loves it almost as much as she loves steaming open letters other people have written. Unfortunately, Mother's letters are what people call "poison pen." Mother doesn't call them that, of course. She thinks of her letter writing as a sacred duty. Too often I've heard her say, "Someone should drop that woman a line and tell her just how low she is—copying that song like that. It's my duty as your mother to do it. I *will* do it." Then Mother would get that too-innocent look in her eye and she would say, "Of course I won't sign it. I'll send it anonymously."

Mother was wearing her letter-writing face as I took her arm and led her away from the weeping woman. She turned back and waved at the woman. Then she wheezed again.

"You know, Louise, I think this fire has brought on an asthma attack." In the same tone she went on to tell me about the weeping woman. "Poor soul, that trailer was all she had in the world. She just arrived this afternoon, and then to have this happen to her! She had a beauty shop in it and used to go around giving permanents and things. She had three steady customers waiting for treatments and there she is, burned out of . . ."

"Mother," I said. "Where were you during the fire?"

"Don't be rude. I was telling you about poor Mrs. Smith. She told me she . . ."

"I don't want to know about her," I said. "I asked you where you were during the fire. Your bed wasn't even slept in."

Even as Mother started explaining, I was sorry I had asked. It was too easy to remember Mother's words: *leave everything to me.* Too easy to remember how Mother remedied situations.

"Mother, did you start that fire?"

Her blue eyes looked at me calmly. Her face was flushed. I hoped the flush was from the asthma, but in my heart I knew better.

"Why, Louise! How can you ask me a thing like that? Your own mother!"

Then I knew it was true. But why did she do it? I didn't ask her; I was afraid of the answer.

"Oh, stop talking so tragic," Mother said impatiently. "Of course I started the silly old fire. How was I to know that poor woman's trailer would get burned up? And how did you think I could get everybody out of our trailer unless I did something drastic?" Mother tossed her head in anger. "You certainly didn't want those friends of yours to know we were carting a dead body around, did you? You couldn't have dragged it around in the broad daylight, could you? That's the trouble with you and Biff. You have no gratitude."

It wasn't the first time I had been staggered with Mother's methods. I had been through a series of them since I started in show business as a kid, but nothing like this!

"If you'd been the right kind of daughter, you would have helped me," Mother said. "But no!" Then she became more cheerful. "Well, anyway, there's nothing left to worry about. No one got hurt. Nothing got damaged but a few old trees and that trailer of Mrs. Smith's. She has it completely covered by insurance, and the body's buried away just as nice as you could ask for. The . . ."

"No!" The word burst from me. "But—who—helped you?"

"Why, no one." Mother sounded a little hurt that I thought she needed help. "I just waited until everybody was quiet. Then I got out of the car by the back door and found the shovel. I dug a nice hole. Then I started the fire before I went back for the corpse. The hole isn't very deep, though. I do think the very least Biff can do is dig a deeper one. Of course, if we leave town right away, it might not matter. What do you think?"

"Did anyone see you?"

"See me when?"

"When you were burying the body," I said as patiently as my trembling voice would allow.

Mother stopped walking for a moment. "You know," she said slowly, "now that you mention it, I did think someone was following me. It was when I was pulling the wagon over the bumps . . ."

"What wagon?"

"Why, little Johnny's wagon. You know, the nice family that lives next door to us. The husband is in the scissor-grinding business. Goes from town to town grinding scissors. She's having another baby, too. Three already and another one on the way. It's disgraceful."

"Why that wagon, Mother?"

"Well, we don't own one, and you certainly didn't expect me to carry that corpse over my shoulder, did you?"

Mother was silent a moment. We walked on toward the trailer.

"You know, Louise, I do believe my asthma has cleared up by itself. It's either that new medicine or this dry climate." Mother breathed deeply and clearly.

"Yes," she said. "It certainly has. Oh, by the way, dear, let's not tell Biff about the body right now. Let's wait until later and surprise him."

3 BY SEVEN THAT MORNING THE LAST FIREMAN HAD left and the trailer camp settled down to sleep again. The smell of burnt brush and chemicals coming from the woods was like a badly kept Turkish bath, but my nose had been subjected to such a variety of odors during the last week that it was losing its sensitivity. Anyway, I kept it close to the pot of coffee that was boiling away on the relief stove, so the smell didn't bother me as much as it did Biff.

He divided his complaints between the smell and a blister on his hand. I rather liked the blister. It made him look as though he worked for a living, but I did agree with him about the air.

"Smells like something Bill might have dragged into the trailer," Biff said. Then he started laughing. "Boy, if this isn't one for the book!"

His laugh sounded dirty to me. I glanced up from the coffeepot, and that made him laugh louder.

"Punkin, you ought to see yourself," he said. "You lost half your eyebrows."

I don't see anything funny about that to this day. I *had* lost half my eyebrows and my bangs were singed. Not only that, my hair was gray with smoke. So were my clothes.

"I don't think that's very kind of you," I said in a martyred tone. "Laughing at me when I'm bending over this hot stove making coffee for *you*. I could very nicely have used the time putting on full makeup, and, anyway, if you think you're Rembrandt!"

Biff rattled the cups and saucers around on the table and brought the can of milk from the extra icebox on the running board of the trailer. By then I was beginning to think the setup was funny, too, that is, everything but my singed eyebrows.

"You were wonderful, honey," I said offhand-like. "Thinking about digging the trench and everything. I certainly didn't see anyone else working so hard," I stirred the coffee vigorously. No sense in letting him think he was *too* wonderful, I decided.

"You were pretty swell yourself," Biff was just as offhand. "Driving the car away and pouring water and . . . Say! Where is the car?"

In all the excitement I had forgotten it myself. Then I remembered I had left the animals in it.

"It's down the road a ways," I said. "Have your coffee first. Then go get it. While your gone I'll fix the dogs' breakfast."

"Punkin, the Personality Girl of the Old Opera, making breakfast!" Biff said it comfortably. He settled back in the chair and lit two cigarettes, one for me. "I bet if I told the boys they'd never believe it. Here you are, living in a trailer camp in Ysleta, Texas. Corpse in the bathtub, fire in the woods, everything you need to start light housekeeping. And me with a blister on my hand yet. A blister from a shovel!"

Biff caressed the blister and let a dreamy light fill his eyes. I knew what he was thinking. He was visualizing the story in newspaper print. That's the only trouble with marrying in the business—no secrets.

The no secrets reminded me of my own secret. I hadn't had a chance to tell Biff about Mother's excursion into the woods, and he looked so pleased with life in general that I didn't have the heart to spoil things. Not until we'd had our coffee, anyway. I had no intentions of surprising him as Mother suggested, but it was a difficult subject to bring up. We hadn't been married long enough for me to say, "Look, dear, Mother did the damnedest thing. She set fire to the woods so she could bury the body."

As far as that goes, we hadn't been married at all. Not if you want to be technical about it. We had a deep-sea captain say the right words, and I wore the ring on the right finger, but since the night of our marriage we hadn't been alone for five minutes.

It wasn't only Mother and our guests. Even before they joined us, the studio had sent a publicity man as chaperone until we went through another ceremony that would sound legal to the Hays office. They didn't like the water-taxi business. They didn't like the idea of our captain being willing to disregard the technicalities of a marriage license, and they didn't like me particularly to start with. Making a movie actress out of a burlesque queen was a tougher job than they had anticipated.

Hays organization or no Hays organization, I had no intentions of spoiling my romantic marriage. My father had been married at sea; my grandfather had been married at sea, and I had an uncle who married himself at sea. I was being traditional, and if they wanted to call it living in sin, it was all right with me. One thing sure: they weren't going to get me to wear a white veil and have doves flying around while an organ played bad music. I wasn't exactly suspended by my studio, but I was too close to it for comfort. I knew I could always go back to burlesque.

"Punkin?"

"What?"

"What were you thinking about?"

"Honest? Or can I color it a little?"

"Honest," Biff said.

"I was thinking if this is living in sin it sure is overrated."

When Biff smiles he's rather handsome. He smiled then, an

extra-nice smile. He got up and dropped an eggshell into the coffeepot, and I thought he looked substantial, standing there in the early-morning sunlight.

He's a little too tall, six feet four, and because he's always been conscious of his height, he stoops. Just in the knees, though. Most people think he stoops because it gets a laugh on his theater entrances, but that isn't true. His hair is dark and, with the exception of one lock that stands straight up in the back, it's wavy. His eyes are a real Irish blue, almost black when he's angry, and I like his mouth. It's big, but, like Mother says, a big mouth is a sign of generosity. She doesn't say that about Biff's mouth, of course. On him a big mouth means deceit. If he'd been anything but an actor he could have gotten away with no mouth at all, but Mother doesn't like actors. Least of all she likes burlesque actors.

"Having fun?" he asked me.

"Uh-huh. Best honeymoon I ever had."

Biff placed the cups on the table. He looked closely at one and began polishing it with Mother's asthma towel. "Mandy's getting damn careless with his dishwashing," he said.

"Well, at least he tries," I said. "That's more than I can say for that Corny friend of yours. Do you know he wasn't even around last night when that fire was . . ."

The car driving up interrupted me. With a screeching of brakes it stopped a few feet from the table. It was our car, and Corny scrambled out of the backseat. His pajamas were wrinkled, but I was glad to see he had on the bottoms even if they didn't match the tops. His eyes were bleary. I glared at him as he staggered over to the table and reached for the bottle of Wilson's.

"I'll have one of those brown boys," he said.

"You've had enough brown boys to populate South Africa," I snapped, taking the bottle from his hand. "Go to bed and sleep it off. On the floor for once."

Corny didn't move. He glowered at me as though he couldn't make up his mind whether to hit me on the head or kick me in the teeth.

"Where've you been?" Biff asked.

"Where do you think I'd be?" Corny said. "Hanging around here making a damn-fool hero out of myself? Where there is smoke there is no Cliff Corny Cobb. I went into town and had me a couple of snorts, that's where I been.'

"You've got a helluva nerve taking our car out when you're drinking," I said. Then I remembered where I had left the car. "How did you know where it was, anyway?"

Corny had to brace himself against the tent pole to keep from falling flat on his face. I had never seen him that tight.

"If you must know," he said, "I was walking into town and I passed the car down the road. You shouldn'ta left the keys if you don't want nobody but yourself to drive it. And don't go talking about me having my nerve . . ."

Then I saw that Corny wasn't alone. A man was getting out of the driver's seat of the car. He was the biggest man I'd ever seen. Not that he was taller than Biff; it was a different kind of bigness. He had big hands, a big head with lots of curly, almost gray hair on it. His eyebrows were bushy and his ears were big, too. When he walked into the sunlight I could see that he needed a shave.

Biff poured him a drink. The man had that kind of face. You wanted to drink with him even before you knew him.

"Kind of early for actors to be up, ain't it?"

His voice was exactly what I'd expected. It was big and boomy. He looked and sounded like a perfect ad for Texas. He pulled up a camp chair and sat facing Biff. "This is the most excitement Yselta's had since I been sheriff. A fire and actors all at once. We don't get many stage actors around here. Last one we had was away back—some cowboy with false teeth."

The sheriff took the drink from Biff and downed it in one gulp. He wiped his mouth with the back of his hand.

"Do you want a chaser?" I asked.

Biff didn't give him a chance to answer. "Chaser, hell," he said, digging up a gag from the bottom of the trunk. "Nothing can catch that last one."

I was glad the sheriff ignored the dialogue. He was still thinking about his cowboy with the store-bought china.

"No, sir," the sheriff said, slapping his thigh. "That cowboy didn't know one end of a horse from the other."

That was his contribution to the floor show and he laughed heartily.

I tried to laugh with him, but it was an effort. If I hadn't known he was the sheriff it would have been a cinch, but between the doubt of our corpse half-buried in the woods and Corny's sly looks, I just couldn't get with it.

Suddenly the sheriff stood up. He sauntered over to the trailer and peered through the screen door.

"All them folks in there actors?" he asked, as though such a thing were impossible. Then he wrinkled up his nose. "Boy, they sure do stink!"

Biff hurried over and tried to explain the odor. "Oh, that's Evangie's asthma powder. That's my mother-in-law and she's got . . ."

"Whatever she's got," the sheriff interrupted, "we bury 'em in Texas when they smell better'n that."

Biff raised one eyebrow. "That's my gag," he said. "I broke it at the Gaiety. You must get around, brother."

The sheriff smiled. He walked back to me and scribbled a name and number on a piece of paper.

"That's Dr. Gonzales' number. He's got some kind of injections for asthma. Allergies, I think he calls 'em. Tell him you're friends of mine."

Before I had time to read the number, the sheriff took the paper away from me. "Here," he said. "I'll put my number down, too, just in case you need me."

I glanced at the number without seeing the names or numbers. Why, I thought, would the sheriff think we needed him?

He was having another drink with Biff. "Up the river," they said in chorus. The sheriff had another drink. Then he turned to leave. He refused Biff's offer of a lift into town.

"Nope. Like to walk when I get the chance. Speaking of driving, though, better not let this friend of yours at the wheel anymore. He busted the hell outta the rear end of your car." The sheriff looked Corny over from head to foot. It wasn't a love look. "He's a little too mouthy for the size of him, anyway."

Biff and I waited until the sheriff was out of sight before we examined the car. The sheriff was right. Not only was the rear end smashed, but the trailer hitch was snatched off clean.

"Some drunk backed inta me," Corny said insolently.

I knew he was lying. I only hoped Biff realized it.

"What did that guy mean about your big mouth?" Biff asked.

Corny didn't answer right away. He looked at me and grinned. "Ask her," he said, tossing a thumb in my direction.

"I ain't asking anybody but you." Biff was calm, but his eyes were getting blacker every second. "What's more, I don't like your attitude. Pack your toothbrush, funny boy. You and me have come to the end of a beautiful friendship."

My first feeling was that it was almost worthwhile. If it took a corpse and a brush fire to get rid of that sponger, I'd sit still for both. My second feeling wasn't as easy. Corny's lips had turned up in a smile. He rocked back and forth on his unsteady legs.

"You mean you want me to leave this happy little group?" he asked. "Well, brother, you are asking the wrong guy. From a few hours ago I am already the star boarder." He turned to go into the trailer and, as an afterthought, he patted me one on the back. "Ask your dear little mother what she was doing during the fire," he said.

Biff grabbed him by the seat of his pajamas before Corny knew what had happened to him. He pulled him off the step and shook him around.

"Apologize to my wife!" Biff said.

I've always dreamed of a moment like that. The dialogue was usually, "Unhand that woman!" In my dreams I had rehearsed myself to go into a womanly act, but when I came face to face with the scene, I didn't like it at all. It made me feel foolish. I didn't know whether to frown with great dignity or smile with great generosity. I took the middle road.

"You're both nuts," I said, and walked away. I stumbled over the guy ropes that held the lean-to, but I didn't care. My mind wasn't on big exits.

Of all the people in the world, Cliff Corny Cobb would be the one to see mother bury the body. When I got behind the trailer, I said, "Dammit!" It made me feel better, so I said it again. "Dammit."

"Maybe he didn't though," I said aloud. "After all, he was walking in the other direction, or he wouldn't have found the car. He did go into the village, or he wouldn't have met the sheriff."

I felt in my pocket for the scrap of paper with the Sheriff's name and address on it, then continued arguing with myself. "I think we'd better talk this over with him right now."

Biff interrupted me. "What's with the solo back here?"

"I was talking to myself," I said. "Look, honey, let's go into town right now and get the car fixed. I'd like to get out of this town, and quick."

Biff put his arm around me, and we walked toward the car.

"What did that guy mean when he said ask you what your mother was doing during the fire?"

Biff's voice sounded casual. I tried to keep mine that way, too.

"I'll tell you later. After we get the car fixed."

"With what I expect from the local garage setup," Biff said, "I will be wearing a long gray beard and listening through an ear trumpet."

4 THE GARAGE MAN WAS ON HIS BACK UNDER THE car. "Well, it'll take three or four days. Gotta be welded, you know," he said. "We don't get many repair jobs like this and we may have to make a new part."

Biff and I started to speak at the same time. Because I'm the female side of the house, he let me go first.

"Does it look like it was done purposely?" I asked.

The garage man moved back and forth on his roller machine. I let him play for a minute. Then I told him to stop clowning and get up and look where I was looking. I pointed out the clean break in the hitch. "There," I said. "Does that look like it's been sawed or something?"

The mechanic scratched his head. "Maybe, but who'd want to do a thing like that?"

I didn't bother telling him about my husband's very good friend. It was just as well, too, because, after thinking it over, I decided that even if Corny had seen Mother bury the body, there would be no point in smashing up the car. Unless he wanted us to stay in Ysleta, and that didn't seem to make sense.

"That's cast iron," the mechanic was saying to Biff. "You know how that snaps? Almost always clean . . ."

Biff waited patiently while the man explained all about metals, semiprecious and otherwise. The he asked him if there was a bar in town.

The mechanic pointed a greasy hand to the side street. My eyes followed the hand.

A bar? There were nothing but bars: The Blinking Pup, The Red Mill, The Last Hole. As far as I could see the signs read BAR and BEER.

"Have you any other industries here in Ysleta?" Biff asked.

The mechanic finally got the joke. "Hah!" he said. "It's because we're so close to the border. Lots of tourists want a nightcap when the bridge to Mexico closes. Closed up tighter than a drum over there, but we're wide open."

Biff cast an eye over the street. "No kidding?"

We picked out one of the livelier-looking bars, The Happy Hour, and stopped in for a beer. Biff picked up a bottle of Wilson's, and we were ready to leave. A clock over the door indicated that it was ten after one.

"Better bring home a couple containers of beer," I suggested. Our family'll be getting up, and when they know we're stuck here for a few days, they'll want a bracer. Better make it another bottle of rye," I added after a second's consideration. "Beer won't handle it."

While we waited for the bartender to stop picking his teeth, four musicians straggled wearily to the small stage in back of the saloon. They played two choruses of Amapola and suddenly, from out of nowhere, six chorus girls came galloping out onto the floor.

They were the tiredest-looking chorus girls I've ever seen, and, being in burlesque for years, I've seen them tired. These wore abbreviated lavender rayon panties and net brassieres. They carried stringy white fans and waved them around listlessly.

Biff looked at the clock again. Then he looked around the saloon. There wasn't a customer in the place unless you could count us and one very dark little man who sat alone in a booth near the stage. He had a split of champagne in front of him and not once during the girl's routine did he look up.

"Is this the beginning of a new day," Biff asked the bartender, "or is it a leftover from last night?"

The bartender shrugged his shoulders. "Guess it's a rehearsal. I'm a stranger here myself."

I looked back to the floor show. The girls were making a rose with their fans. The only way I recognized it as a rose was that in burlesque we did the same routine. The rose was at the bud stage when a piece of pink cheesecloth emerged from the side of the stage.

There was something under it, of course, and when the rose became full-blown, we not only got a glimpse of what the something was but it was enough to make me grab the bottle from the bartender's hands and start a mad dash for the door.

Biff had always been considered the Casanova of burlesque. I took that into consideration when I married him, and we were usually running into his ex-flames. But I never expected to find one under a piece of cheesecloth in Ysleta, Texas!

Biff stared at the dancer with his mouth half-open. Then he grinned at her, finally at me. "It's a small world, ain't it?" he asked when she tossed her brassiere on the piano.

I waited until she threw her G-string into the tuba to answer. "Indeed it is," I replied.

We had been too busy watching the show to see the little

dark man get up from the booth. He stood next to Biff with a cigar in his mouth. The cigar was unlit, and the little man rocked back and forth on his heels.

"You likea the show?" he asked.

Biff jumped a foot in the air. He had to look down around his elbow to find where the voice came from.

The little man didn't seem to be too pleased. Maybe it was because Biff gave him a double take. I was afraid Biff was warming up for a joke like "Get out of the hole," or "Get off your knees." He was too surprised to be a comic, though.

He watched the man pull a card case from his yellow vest and he stared at the man's hands. I didn't blame him for that. They were brown hands, and black hairs grew in little mountains on each knuckle. The fingernails were bright pink, very shiny, with black tips.

"I owna these place," the man said while Biff read the card.

I looked over Biff's shoulder. FRANCISCO CULLICIO, the card read, DEALER IN FINE PERFUMES, LINENS, LIQUORS.

"I gotta getta me some new cards," the man explained, "now that I'ma in the show business."

Biff and I grinned at him broadly.

He didn't smile back. He had stopped rocking on his heels but he had gone into another annoying little piece of business. He snapped a cigar cutter. He still hadn't looked toward the stage, and the woman dancing around in nothing but a three-inch piece of adhesive plaster was getting annoyed.

With a corny toss of her head she finished her number and threw her hands above her head, the same way she used to finish when she was in burlesque.

The new impresario watched me smile woodenly at my naked friend.

"She'sa good, eh?"

"If you like that sort of thing," I replied coldly.

"I puta her to work. Womans costa too much money. All the time she's askin' me for money, so I say sure, I give you twenty fi' a week, only you work for it."

He snapped his cigar cutter a few times. I think I was supposed to be impressed with the salary. I gave him a dead pan, so he went on.

"Course, she geta more than twenty fi' a week. She geta fi' cents every drink."

Well, I thought to myself, that runs into a tidy sum, considering the way she guzzles. Then something slowly dawned on me.

"You mean she gets five cents for every drink she drinks with a customer?"

Cullucio didn't answer me. He was too busy watching Biff.

One glimpse of my husband-of-a-week and I began to wonder if it wouldn't have been smarter to point the trailer toward Reno. He was almost a part of the floor show, waving his arms like a windmill and pointing to the empty stool next to us.

"You can send a card backstage, ya know," I said.

There was no response, just a more vigorous waving of arms.

"Why don't you go over and talk to the lady?" I asked.

My voice must have been a little louder than I thought, because the dancer looked at me and smiled. I remember that smile; it was a cross between hypophrenic and a brooding cobra.

"She's coming out for a drink," Biff said after she made her exit.

I gave him my long, slow look and mumbled, "I can't wait."

For the next half hour my job was to keep Cullucio from pinning Biff's ears back. He could have handled it himself, but, between his bartender and the beefy man at the door, Biff was a dead pigeon.

It isn't that Biff is mentally deficient or anything; he's just too trusting. From the moment that Joyce Janice sat on the bar stool next to us I knew the score. She and the little dark man were splitting their room rent. To me it's in black and white, but Biff doesn't catch. He listens intently to her life story and keeps pouring drinks down her throat.

At a nickel each, she was building up a nice little nest egg for herself, I thought. Not that she was going to be able to keep it. The heavy breathing of my friend with the pink fingernails told me that the money would go for hospital bills.

"Come on out of the house for dinner," Biff said for the four-teenth time.

Joyce said no again. "We never know when a live one might drop in, then we gotta do another show."

"I thought this was a rehearsal," Biff said. "The bartender—"

"He's nuts," Joyce said. "This is our tea dance. We do 'em twice a week."

She was wearing a blue-satin evening gown, and every time she leaned over it was show enough—hardly the costume for a tea dance, but Biff had been in burlesque too long to notice it. The bartender, though, was having himself a time.

I tried to tell myself that Biff was just being sociable, that he felt rather sorry for Joyce. It wasn't too hard to feel sorry for her. Her silver shoes were worn down at the heels, perspiration had stained her gown almost to her hips, and she had a black-and-blue mark the size of a Mexican peso on her flabby arm.

She didn't seem to feel uncomfortable, though. She knew Cullucio was burning and she liked being the center of atten-tion. She kept track of the drinks by scratching a mark with her fingernail on the top of the bar.

On the tenth scratch I got to my feet. I tapped Biff on the shoulder. "End of joke," I said sweetly. "Unless you'd like to stay here alone." On the alone line I stared straight at Joyce.

The same clock said three forty-five when Biff tore himself away from The Happy Hour. We didn't speak while he settled the check. The walk to the trailer camp was silent, too.

It wasn't that I was jealous or—oh, well, I may as well admit it. I was jealous, and annoyed, and my feet hurt and my head ached. It certainly wasn't the time to tell Biff about Mother, but I did. He looked too complacent. Why should I be the only one to worry, I thought.

"Oh, by the way," I said casually. "Mother wants you to dig a deeper hole. She buried the body last night."

We walked on a few feet. Biff had a complacent gleam in his eye.

"She set fire to the woods. I think that's what Corny meant when he said . . ."

We walked a few feet more, and suddenly Biff stopped. He stopped so suddenly he almost lost his balance. I grabbed the box of eggs from him just in time.

"She *what*?"

I couldn't have been more casual if I'd said she took out the furniture so she could sweep under the beds. I walked on toward the trailer. If I could whistle I would have whistled.

I said, "She set fire to the woods so she could get the body out of the trailer."

5 GEE GEE AND MANDY WERE PLAYING CARDS WHEN we got home. I put the food in the icebox, and Biff, with a dazed look in his eye, began fixing the drinks.

Dimples heard the clink of the glasses and came out of the trailer. She was still wearing her kimono, a faded-pink affair with a marabou trimming. Her head was covered with a Turkish towel, and little flakes of white henna were on her forehead.

"Where in hell was you so long?" she asked. Then she saw the bottles, and her petulant mouth relaxed. She walked down the steps, being very careful not to trip. One heel of her mules was loose and she had to be careful. The grayish pompoms dragged in the dust as she made her way to the camp chair. She had her manicuring set with her and she placed it on the table, leaving room for the bottle and glasses.

"Where's Mother?" I asked.

Gee Gee tossed a finger toward the burned trailer, and I saw Mother. She was walking with her arm around the woman who had been crying the night before.

"That's Mrs. Smith," Gee Gee said. "Her husband died, and she used his insurance money to buy the trailer. She had a beauty shop in it and she traveled around giving permanents and stuff. You know how sympathetic Evangie is? Well, when the poor old dame gets burned out, your mother makes room for her with us. She's in the front seat of the car for tonight, but Evangie is fixing a place for her in the bedroom."

Gee Gee didn't look at me while she was talking. She busied herself with getting the glasses. She put her hand to her mouth, then she bit her thumbnail. Finally she burst out, "Oh, Gyp, I can't tell you what we been through this morning. Your mother has the whole camp in an uproar. Everybody's gonna sue. Don't ask me who they're gonna sue, but Evangie's convinced 'em that the city is responsible for the fire, negligence or somethin'. They been holding a council of war since noon."

Biff opened his mouth to say something. Then he saw Mother and changed his mind.

She was waving gaily as she passed one trailer after another. She stopped at one to inquire about the health of "little Johnny."

I looked at Gee Gee.

"That's their kid, and he wouldn't eat his Pablum until Evangie told him a story."

Mother's stories are enough to give little Johnny permanent indigestion. I wondered if she told him the one about the woman throwing her eleven children to the wolves, or the one about the man cutting off his wife's head with a meat ax. They were Mother's favorites.

"Does Johnny have a wagon?" I asked Gee Gee.

Gee Gee shrugged her shoulders. She was looking at Mother again. The sun on Mother's hair brought out the highlights and the sky made her eyes seem bluer than ever.

"No wonder she's such a spellbinder," Gee Gee said, as Mother walked toward us.

She was lovely, I thought with pride.

"Where were you, dear?" Mother asked happily. Before I had a chance to tell her, she thrust Mrs. Smith under my nose, introduced her, and then whispered, "She's had so much trouble, Louise. Be nice to her."

It would have been difficult to be otherwise. Mrs. Smith looked as if she'd had trouble. When she came closer I could see the deep wrinkles in her leathery face, the faded blue of her eyes, the lifelessness of her badly marcelled hair. She couldn't have been much older than Mother, but as they stood together Mother was radiant in comparison.

I told Mrs. Smith that we were very happy to have her with us until she could find more comfortable quarters, and she burst out crying.

"You've all been so wonderful to me," she sobbed. "I never knew people like you before."

Mother put her arm around the woman's thin shoulder. "Now, Mamie, don't cry. Everything is going to be all right."

Biff offered the crying woman a drink, but Mother scowled and shook her head. "And you've had about enough, too," she said, leading Mamie into the trailer.

When they opened the screen door, all the dogs started barking at once and Cliff piled out the back door.

"Can't a guy get any sleep around here?" he complained as he fell into a chair.

"It's three-thirty. If you wanta sleep, go to a hotel." Gee Gee pushed a cup of coffee under his face and banged the silver around noisily. "I've been trying to clean up in there since twelve this afternoon," she added.

Gee Gee's idea of cleaning up was to kick things around until they got lost, but she meant well. Biff usually did the heavy scrubbing, Mother helped me with the cooking. Dimples did the beds, and Mandy was dishwasher. Corny stood around and got in everybody's way. He was hungover but not remorseful. When Biff asked him where he got the load, he said The Happy Hour, and then shut up.

He knew Joyce Janice. They'd played the Eltinge together just a few seasons ago. I thought it rather strange that he didn't mention seeing her at the saloon. Then I had another idea. It could be that he was too drunk to see anyone. I didn't ask him about the broken hitch; I knew he'd lie about it regardless. But I did ask him how he found the sheriff.

"He was hanging around the bar, and when I had trouble getting the car started, he said he'd drive me." Corny went back to blowing on his coffee and finished drinking it before he said, "I thought you might want to see him. I'm sure he'd be interested in what your mother was doing with that shovel last night. Handled it pretty good, too."

Corny reached for the bottle and poured himself a stiff drink. Then he lit a cigarette and leaned back in the camp chair. He blew a smoke ring and stuck his finger through it.

"It'd look like hell in the papers, wouldn't it?" he asked quietly.

"What'd look like hell in what papers?" Biff asked.

Corny drank his rye and didn't answer.

He didn't have to. I knew the answer.

Corny and Biff started out in burlesque the same season. Corny went straight to the top. He was first comic, Biff was second. Corny got the billing, Biff got nothing. Corny got the salary. Biff got peanuts. Then suddenly Biff's break arrived. Not just recognition in burlesque, but a made-to-order part in a Broadway show. I knew how Biff's success rankled in Corny's heart. I knew, too, that Corny would never be satisfied until Biff was back in burlesque as a second comic.

Biff took my arm firmly. "Come on, Gyps. We're going to the village again."

I would like to have put on at least half a face, but with no makeup, my hair in strings, and still wearing the dirty slacks, I allowed myself to be carried off to Ysleta.

Biff didn't loosen his hold on me until we were off the camp grounds. When we passed the last trailer I took out my compact and tried to do something with my face. It was useless.

"Look, darling," I said, putting the compact back into my pocket, "I don't mind having the natives get a preview of how I look when I wake up in the morning, but I would like to know what is the rush. That is, if I'm not being too obtrusive, as Mother would say."

Biff didn't even have the courtesy to look at me. With his eyes straight ahead, he replied slowly, "Career or no career, mother-in-law or no mother-in-law, murder is murder. I love your mother. You know that, but . . ."

"Skip the buildup and give me the meat of the dialogue," I interrupted.

"Well," Biff said after he had sulked a little, "you'll have to admit that Evangie can be difficult at times. If Corny did know anything . . ."

"*If?*"

"Yeah, he probably saw Evangie with the shovel heading for the woods. But if he was sure what she was doing, I think he would have come right out and said it."

We walked on awhile without talking. Then Biff grinned.

"It was kinda cute of her at that. All by herself dragging that putrid old body into the woods and burying it. They don't make women like that today."

I should have let it go at that, but not me! Oh no, I'm always in there with my big mouth wide open. I had to tell him about my great great grandmother.

"She was a part of the Donner expedition, ya know."

Biff gave me a "really," so I went into the story headfirst.

"Yeah. They were homesteading and they got lost in the mountains in the winter. Snow and wolves and no food. It must have been terrible. My grandmother was one of the few survivors. Grandpa used to tell me how the scouts found her. She was in a daze, of course, and her ears were frozen, but she looked so fat and healthy they couldn't figure the thing out. By all rights she shoulda been damn near starved to death, lost for over a month like that. But not my great great grandmother! When they got her home and undressed her, what do you think they found?"

"I dunno," Biff said disinterestedly.

"Steaks, all strapped around her body. Human steaks."

I kept on walking but I peeked at Biff from the corner of my eye. He was still staring straight ahead, so I gave him the black-out. "They recognized one piece of the meat as my great great uncle Louie. They could tell by the tattoo on his hip. It was a picture of the rock of ages. I was named after him; you know, Louie, Louise."

There was more to the story, but Biff made a dive for the bushes. I waited for him. I thought it was the wifely thing to do. When he came out, he was white around the eyes, so I didn't tell him about my great great grandfather. I suddenly realized I'd better give Biff the family history character by character.

We walked the next half mile silently. Then Biff's complexion cleared a little. "Real pioneer stock," he said. "Yep, that accounts for it."

6 WE FOUND THE SHERIFF IN HIS OFFICE. HE WAS relaxed in a swivel chair, with his feet, in their high-heeled boots, propped up on the roll-top desk. He put down a copy of *Variety* when Biff and I walked in. Then he stood up to greet us.

"Well, well, I didn't expect to see you so soon," he said jovially. He drew out a chair for me and one for Biff. Then he pulled out a bottle from a drawer in his desk. He poured three drinks into paper cups and placed them in front of us.

"First of all," he said, "we get sociable."

Biff gulped his drink.

I nursed mine.

"Come on, drink up," the sheriff said. "You two look like a couple of beat coyotes. Nothing serious enough for such long faces."

"I'm afraid this is," Biff said.

"If it's about the fire, I was fixing to ask you a few questions," the sheriff said. "Matter of fact, I was going to question you this morning. Then, when I saw that you really were a bunch of actors, I didn't bother."

Biff sat on the edge of his chair. His expression was the same as when H. I. Moss would ask him to take a salary cut. Biff always knew he'd agree to the terms, but he liked to be coaxed.

I knew he was going to tell everything, but he wanted to wait for the right moment.

He didn't have to wait long. The sheriff must have gone to the same school of acting. His timing was beautiful.

"Yep," he said. "Soon's I knew you were actors I knew you wouldn't be mixed up in anything like that."

"Like what?" Biff asked cautiously.

"Why, that body we found in the woods during the fire," the sheriff replied, as though we should know all about it. "Shot through the head. Body was in bad shape, too. Dead for a spell, all right."

I drank my drink on that.

"Yep. Looked like someone poured gasoline on it and then touched it with a match. We'll be able to identify it, but . . ."

"Mother wouldn't do that!" I said.

The sheriff and Biff stared at me. The sheriff in surprise, Biff in annoyance.

"Will you let me tell it, Punkin?" he asked. "You get too involved. And not only that, you keep pulling the blackout too quick. This is the way it happened," Biff said to the sheriff. "Last week we got married. We bought the trailer for our honeymoon. First we send for Evangie so she can go along for the ride. Then we start running into these friends of ours. They're all going east, and so are we. Plenty of room. So we ask 'em . . ."

"You ask 'em, you mean," I said, just in case the sheriff got the wrong idea.

"All right then. I ask them. Anyway, there we are: dogs, monkey, guinea pig, friends, mother-in-law . . ."

"And," I interrupted again, "you might give my mother top billing."

"Bill, our doggie, has developed an annoying habit of dragging presents into the trailer for us," Biff said, ignoring me completely. "One day it's a fish head, next day it's a bone, then it's something we can't name. Anyway, these things have a rare smell to 'em. Evangie's asthma powder has got a rare smell. Between the mixture, we don't notice this other smell until we get in Ysleta yesterday. Then the three of us start looking. We naturally think Bill has come up with a prize, but what we don't expect is what we find.

"Evangie sees it when she opens up the bed in the back room. There's a tin bathtub under it. We don't use the tub because we always stop in tourist camps and they have showers. You have to carry a lot of water for that tub business, and it makes the trailer side heavy. So, we haven't looked under that bed since we left San Diego. Anyway, Evangie lets the bed fall down and then she locks the doors before she tells us what's in the tub. I take a look, and sure enough!"

"There it is," I said.

"The damnedest, deadest body you ever saw."

The sheriff pinched his chin with a large hand. He looked at Biff from under his bushy eyebrows. "A body, eh?"

"Yep," Biff said. "When I go to lift it out of the tub, a hunk of the face fell off."

That's when I spilled my drink. Biff had promised me he would never mention that again. While I told him what I thought of him for going into all the sordid details when he knew very well how sick it made me, the sheriff began talking to himself.

"That fits, all right," he said.

Biff had brought my great great grandmother into the argument, so I didn't get the sheriff's question until he repeated it.

"Did you recognize the body?"

"Oh, sure," Biff said. "He was our best man."

The sheriff thought that meant that we had known him all our lives, so we had to go through the whole story of our water-taxi wedding; how we found the best man in a saloon, how we picked up the captain in another saloon, where we got the boat, and everything.

"Never saw him before, eh?"

"Never," Biff said. "Never saw him after, either. That is, until I lifted up the bed and looked in the bathtub."

"Except that time in San Diego," I said firmly.

Biff shook his head. "Gyp swears she saw the guy in San Diego, but the guy we saw didn't even speak to us. If it'd been George, why he'd have fallen all over us. He was a very pleasant guy."

"George who?" the sheriff asked.

Biff and I looked at each other. That was the first time I had thought about our best man having a last name.

"We didn't ask him," Biff said. "Funny, now that I think it over. You'd think he woulda told us."

"Yes," the sheriff said. "Or that you would have asked him.

Now, what about those other actors traveling with you? Any of them recognize the body?"

"Oh, we didn't let them know what we were trouping around with us," Biff said quickly. "Those two dames would have gone off their nut. Then, too, we thought we should tell the cops first."

"So you waited a day to do that," the sheriff said. "In the meantime someone steals the corpse, carries it out to the woods, pours gasoline on it, and sets it afire . . ."

I knew what was going through Biff's head. It was going through mine, too. The solution sounded good. We hadn't said it. The sheriff said it. If he wanted to reconstruct the scene to please himself, why should we break it up?

"No," Biff said slowly. "Gyp's mother, Evangie, that is . . ."

"Mother set fire to the wood." I said it quickly, before I could change my mind. "Mother did it so she could bury the body. She wouldn't have poured gasoline on it, though. Mother wouldn't do a thing like that."

The sheriff raised an eyebrow. Then he scratched his chin again.

"If anybody but an actor told me a story like that, I wouldn't believe it," he said. "Even with actors, I find it hard to swallow. For instance, why should your mother go to all that bother burying a body when none of you knew the corpse? Why not go right to the police and tell the story? Then another thing. How could you stand the smell of a body decaying right under your bed? Why didn't you ask those four friends of yours about it? And why didn't you tell me about it this morning when I was out there? How could a woman carry a body like that? What kind of a woman could lift it, let alone carry it almost five hundred feet?"

"She put it in a wagon," I said. "You didn't expect her to carry it over your shoulder, did you?" I didn't realize I had used Mother's exact words until they were out of my mouth. "It was a neighbor's wagon," I added lamely.

"And the reason she didn't want to tell the police was because she didn't want Gyp to have all that bad publicity," Biff said.

"Evangie's got a strange way of justifying things. She figured that as long as we didn't kill the guy, why should we go through the mess of being suspected maybe. Hell's bells, the guy was dead. There was nothing we could do about that. Then why tell the bunch that's traveling with us? Telling them would be like broadcasting it over a national hookup. I'll be damned if I can explain why we didn't get wise to the odor, though. It may be because the bathtub adjoins the icebox. There's only one drain, ya see. Maybe the ice kept the body chilled."

"In other words," the sheriff said, "you condone this act of your mother-in-law's?"

"Not exactly," Biff replied. "But she is my mother–in-law. I gotta stick by her, don't I? And she really was doing it for Punkin and me."

The sheriff got to his feet slowly. He reached over and took his hat from an antler hanging on the wall. "Think you could find the burial place?" he asked me.

"I know the general direction," I said.

The sheriff looked at Biff and me for a moment. Then he threw open the door. The bright sunlight blinded me. Then I saw the Model T parked in front of us.

The sheriff climbed into the front seat. "Well, come on," he said. "Let's go take a look at where your mother buried that body of hers."

Biff climbed into the front seat with the sheriff. I sat in the back. The sheriff, I decided, was certainly not squandering the taxpayers' money. I have traveled in broken-down crates before, but the sheriff's car was a new experience in discomfort. It was no time to beef, though, so I kept my ideas to myself.

Instead of driving through the trailer camp, he took a longer route around the back. It brought us out near Mrs. Smith's burned trailer. The sheriff parked the car, and we got out to walk from there.

The dry grass underfoot was dusty and hot. It burned right through my thin-soled sandals. The same heavy smell of chemicals and gasoline filled the air. The trailer looked sad, I thought. Twisted metal supports were mixed up with the remains of a permanent-wave machine. The base of a hair drier was still intact. Otherwise it was a total loss.

"They won't be able to salvage much of that," I said. I thought I had been talking to Biff, but when I turned around he had disappeared. I called his name, and he answered from the burned wreckage.

"I was just casing the joint," he said as he caught up with me. "You never know what women suffer for their kissers until you take a look at those contraptions. Can you imagine a guy going through all that to get a good looking?"

"In some cases," I said "it might help a little."

The sheriff walked on ahead, so we followed him. The ground was hot. Not from the sun now but from the fire. Here the grass was charred and still smoking in places. The small tree stumps had been uprooted by the firemen and they looked like wires reaching up through the black dirt.

Ahead, I saw the disturbed grave. The shallow hole was empty.

"Looks like a woman's idea of a deep hole," the sheriff said. He kicked aside a few leaves that were under his foot.

Biff stood near him and peered into the hole. They both reached for the white square of linen at the same time.

The sheriff was quicker. He held a handkerchief in his hands. It was a plain white handkerchief, the kind you buy in drug-stores for a dime. He shoved it into his pocket before I could see if it was large or small, before I could see if it had a laundry mark on it. Not that I know one laundry mark from another, but I was anxious to know about the handkerchiefs found in the grave. It was clean. I had an idea it had been dropped there since the fire. Mother's handkerchiefs were gaily colored. They were very small.

Biff was looking farther into the woods. He squinted his eyes.

"Look!" he said.

The sheriff and I looked. A six-by-two mound is unmistakable. The dirt that formed the mound was fresh. Even from a distance of several feet. I could see that it was damp.

I followed Biff and the sheriff as they ran toward the mound.

When they began kicking away dirt, I closed my eyes tightly. I knew what they were going to find and I couldn't look at another corpse again as long as I lived.

They worked quietly for a minute. Then I heard the sheriff say, "Easy now. I think this is it."

Biff grunted in agreement.

My eyes were pressed together so tightly that I saw green lights, then red lights dancing before me. I put my hands to my eyes and pushed the thumbs tightly against the center of my nose.

Biff said, "Well, I'll be double damned!" He waited a moment. Then, "This ain't our corpse at all!"

"Naturally," the sheriff said calmly. "Yours is at the morgue."

I opened my eyes and saw Biff holding the coat of a very dead man. Slumped way down in the coat I saw the bulge of the body. The sun was filtering through the stunted trees, and I thought something glittered. I looked more closely and saw the handle of a butcher knife. It was sticking out of the man's back. Just an ordinary butcher knife, and most of it was buried in the ruddy material of the coat.

Biff let the body fall back into the overturned grave, and the dead man's face stared up at me. What was left of a face, I should say.

"Someone must have smashed it in," I heard Biff say hoarsely.

"Wish you hadn't been so quick in handling it," the sheriff said. He knelt down and examined the clothes of the dead man. The lining of the coat was torn, the pockets were turned inside out.

"Stripped clean," the sheriff said.

I looked at him. Stripped was a funny word for him to use, I thought. Then I suddenly knew what he meant.

"Someone did that so you couldn't identify him?"

The sheriff didn't answer me. "Call Doc Gonzales," he said. "That's the number I gave you this morning. Tell the doc to get over here right away. And tell him to pick up a couple of the boys. Biff and I'll wait here."

I vaguely remember running through the woods and toward the camp office. I felt the scrap of paper in my slacks pocket. My hands were wet and sticky. The paper seemed to be soggy, too. In a moment I was in the office. A second later I hear the doctor's voice over the telephone.

"Hurry!" I said to him, as though that mattered. "Murdered. Yes, back of the trailer camp . . ." I hung up and braced myself against the wall.

Then I saw Gee Gee. Her face was white and drawn.

"Did they find him?" she asked.

"Biff and the sheriff . . ." I stammered. "We were out in the woods . . ."

"They took it out of the bathtub?" Gee Gee asked. Little beads of sweat stood out on her forehead. Her red hair was wet where it fell over her neck and shoulders. Her mouth was quivering.

I grabbed her by the arm and began shaking her. "Stop it," I said. "Stop it!"

Suddenly she relaxed.

"How did you know about it?" I asked.

"I – saw it, Gyp," she said. "I saw it in the bathtub yesterday. Oh, Gyppy, what'll I do?" She started crying softly. Her mouth began quivering again. "What'll I do?"

7 IT WASN'T IN THE BATHTUB, IT WAS IN THE WOODS," I said. "And besides, there are two of 'em already. There may be more, for all I know. I do know this new one is a very unpretty thing. Aside from having his face smashed in, someone was being awfully cute when they tore out the tailor label from his coat. They took everything out of the pockets too."

"What about Gus?" Gee Gee asked. Her eyes were wide and frightened, but her mouth had stopped quivering.

"Gus?" I said. "Gus what?"

"Gus is all I know," Gee Gee said. "And all I want to know. He was in the bathtub yesterday. Dead. The dogs were scratching around the bed. I don't know whatever possessed me to lift that mattress, but I did, and that awful face was staring up at me . . ."

Gee Gee buried her face in her hands and began moaning. "I wanted to tell somebody, but every time I got the nerve something'd happen to me and I'd get scared again. I-I knew him, Gyp."

"You couldn't have," I said.

"Yes I did," Gee Gee insisted. "He used to hang around backstage at the Burbank Theater when I was working there. He sold perfume and stuff. I knew it was hot as a pistol because it was so cheap. You know me with stolen stuff. I wouldn't touch it with a ten-foot pole. But plenty of the other kids used to buy from him. I did buy a bottle of Guerlain's Jicky from Mabel, though. She don't tell me where she gets it, just says she's in a mood to sell it cheap. I naturally figure it's a present from some John, so I give her three bucks for it. I get it home and open the bottle and I find out it's junk. The bottle's good but the perfume is like embalming fluid."

"I take it back to Mabel and when I start beefing she tells me to blame Gus, not her, that she got it off him. Only Gus doesn't come around for a while, so I open my big throat and tell the girls what a cheat he is. I get so mad I even tell Max, the cop that's got the theater beat. Then, about a week later, I'm finishing my second act number and the doorman tells me there's a guy in the alley wants to talk to me.

"I throw the skirt of my costume around me and I go out to see who it is. I don't see him right away. He's standing under the fire escape in the dark. Then all of a sudden I feel somebody grab my arm. Naturally, I go to yell and this guy puts his dirty hand over my mouth. 'Shut up, you,' he tells me, 'I hear you been throaty about me around the theater.'

"Then I know who it is. I know it's Gus and I know he's on the warpath about me telling the cop he's selling stolen goods. I'm fixing to tell him to go to hell, but I get a good look at him, and Gyp, there was something about the way he was talking that scared the pants off me. His eyes looked little, like a pig's, and they were red. I got a feeling that he'd just as soon kill me as not. He was telling me to go in and tell the girls I was only kidding about the perfume. I'd look sweet giving him a clean bill of sale after him pushing me around like that! But I don't tell him that. Hell, I just wanted to get rid of him, so I say, 'Sure, I'll tell 'em anything you want.' He says, 'That's a good girl.' Then he shoves something in my hand and runs down the alley.

"I keep watching until I can't see him anymore. Then I go in the prop room, where it's light, so I can get a look at this thing he gave me. It's like a little book, a pamphlet, only it's got the dirtiest pictures in it I ever saw. I've seen pamphlets, but I've never seen anything like that one. There's something else in the book. It's like a cigarette, only it's longer and skinnier. I'm standing there looking at that damn thing and cussing a blue steak to myself when who walks in but Benny the trumpet player. You remember Benny?"

I nodded. I remembered him as a gangly, neurotic musician. Wonderful trumpet player though.

"Well," Gee Gee went on, "Benny takes one look at the cigarette in my hand and he lets out a whoop. 'Look who's joined our club!' he yells. I don't get it. I don't like him much to start out with so I give him a freeze. He looks me up and down real slow. 'Reefing, eh?' he says. Then he turns on his heel and he's gone. Like a hit on the head it comes to me. That Gus has given me a marijuana, Me! Later I find out he's the guy that's been selling 'em around town, to school kids even. He's selling other kinds of dope, too. Cops looking all over for him, and he gives me a marijuana."

Gee Gee pulled out a package of cigarettes and lit two of them. She handed me one, and we smoked silently for a moment.

"I guess I was a dope to go to the cops," she said finally. "I was scared, though. First I went to Max and told him the whole story. He sent me downtown, and I talked to a bunch of plain-clothes guys, Narcotic Squad. They keep asking me questions, and I tell them what I know. I tell them what Gus looks like, how long he's been hanging around the theater. If I'd known it, I'da told 'em what he ate for breakfast, I was that mad. It was a mistake, sure, but how was I to know? Later I find out, of course, I shoulda known he wasn't alone in the racket, but I never would have guessed there were so many guys mixed up with him. First I get the telephone calls. Then guys tap me on the shoulder, notes get slipped under my door, all of 'em telling me to keep my mouth shut or they'll shut it for me permanent. That's one reason I wanted to leave town."

"You should have told Biff and me," I said.

"Oh, sure," Gee Gee said. "You two would have knocked yourselves out asking me to join you. I was just the kid you needed to make your honeymoon complete."

"Did you tell Dimples?" I asked. There wasn't much sense in contradicting her.

"Hell, no," Gee Gee said. "She knew about the perfume of course, because she was working the Burbank when it happened, but I didn't tell a soul about the dope. Oh. Gyp, it's such a mess. What'll I do?"

She began crying again. I put my arms around her and patted her shoulder. In a way I felt like slapping her, but after all she was my friend and she was in trouble. Just because her trouble had become my trouble was no reason for me to get angry with her.

"Look, honey," I said. "Tell the cops the whole story just like you told me. When they know who he was and what he was, they'll probably pin a medal on you for killing him."

Gee Gee pushed me away from her. "But I didn't!" she said hoarsely. "That's why I was afraid to tell anybody his body was in the trailer. I knew they'd think I done it and, so help me, I haven't seen him since that night backstage."

I believed her.

We smoked for a moment longer. Then Gee Gee tossed her cigarette into a fire bucket near the telephone. There was water in the bucket and when the cigarette fell it made a sizzling little noise. There was another sound, though. The sound of someone walking away. I jumped up and ran to the door. It was ajar. I threw it open and looked out. No one was there.

"What was it?" Gee Gee asked listlessly.

"Nothing," I said. "I just thought I heard someone. Must have been the breeze."

Gee Gee didn't question me. We hadn't felt a breeze in a week, but her mind was too occupied to think about that.

"You think the cops will believe me?" Gee Gee asked.

I thought for a moment. I tried to remember the sheriff's expression as he listened to Biff and me. When I did, it wasn't a reassuring picture. I wondered what he would say when he knew that Gee Gee could identify the first corpse, not as a long-shoreman, but as a dope peddler. Then I decided on something.

"Look," I said to Gee Gee. "The sheriff thinks we know the guy you call Gus. We knew him as George; he was our best man. If you go to him now and say it isn't George, it's Gus, the sheriff might think something funny is going on. I don't think *anybody* could tell who the second corpse is, so we don't have to worry about him, why let yourself in for something?"

Gee Gee listened closely. Her head was nodding up and down like one of those counterbalanced doll's heads. Her mouth twitched spasmodically.

"Think you have enough nerve to keep it to yourself?" I asked.

"Gee, Gyp, I don't know . . . I don't know . . ."

"Promise me one thing," I said. I walked over to her and tipped her chin so I could look into her eyes. "If you feel like you're getting ready to spill it, let Biff or me know first. Promise?"

Gee Gee grabbed my hand. "I promise," she said.

"Come on. Let's get ourselves a drink. I'll buy."

Gee Gee got to her feet. She leaned heavily on my arm as we walked toward the trailer. Trailerites were sitting under their awnings having early dinner, and as we passed them they waved good evening to us.

"Some excitement, eh?" one of them shouted with a grin from ear to ear.

"Yes, sir," I shouted back. That trailerite didn't know what excitement was. If he thought a brush fire was excitement, what would he call our two corpses?

Women in slacks and shorts were making the early evening rounds. Children were just warming up for their after-dinner screaming. Here and there a man was washing up at a basin.

It was hard for me to believe that people living in such a close community could be unaware of the two murders.

Our trailer was parked farther away from the center of activity. As Gee Gee and I approached it, Mother closed the bedroom door and started down the steps. She carried a small, carelessly wrapped package in her hand. When I called out to her, she slipped it into her apron pocket.

"Why hello," she said gaily. "Where have you been?"

Gee Gee flopped down into one of the camp chairs; she let her head sink in her hands.

Mother stared at her for a moment. Then she turned to me.

"What's the matter?" she asked. "You look awful. Why don't you fix your hair? Just because you're camping out is no reason to let yourself go like this. I think you're gaining weight, too. I knew this trip would turn out like this. You'll get sunburned and fat, and . . ."

"Biff and I went to see the sheriff," I said. "We went out to the grave and . . ."

Mother looked at me for a long moment, "Well?" she asked.

"We found a body. Not our body, another one."

"Please stop calling it *our* body," Mother said petulantly. "It sounds so—so possessive. How do you know it wasn't ours, anyway?"

"They dug that one up last night," I said. "This new one has a knife in its back."

Mother sat down next to Gee Gee. She arranged her dress carefully over her bare legs and placed her hands on the table. I hadn't expected much animation from her, but I would have liked her to act as though she had heard me.

"Not only that," I said, "but this one had no face."

Mother smiled up at me. "Stop joshing, Louise," she said, "Whoever heard of a corpse without a face?"

I poured some water into the washbasin and doused my head

55

in it. It was cool and it refreshed me. Mother handed me a towel and waited until I dried my face and hands.

"Well, come on," she said. "Let's go look at it."

Gee Gee shivered.

Mother changed her tone. "I mean, let's go see if we can help the police."

"There's no police, Mother, just a sheriff."

"Then we can help the sheriff."

Mother walked ahead of Gee Gee and me. I could see the blue gingham of her dress as she hurried toward the woods. I heard her hum her little tune, "I know a place where the sun never shines . . ."

"Sure you want to go?" I asked Gee Gee. "It isn't pretty, you know."

"I don't give a damn what it looks like so long as I don't recognize him," Gee Gee said.

I suddenly cared, though. I needed fortification to look at it again. I took Gee Gee's arm and led her back to the trailer.

"Let's get that drink we promised ourselves," I said.

Gee Gee got the glasses. I uncovered the bottle, and we had two ryes each. Neat and fast. The trailer was empty. I wondered vaguely where everyone was. Then I felt relieved there was no one around. I was in no mood for casual pleasantries.

Gee Gee and I went back toward the woods.

When we arrived at the burial place, I saw Mother leaning over the grave. The sheriff, hat in hand, was standing next to her.

"I can't say for sure if I know him or not," Mother said. "I don't know who it *could* be. When Louise told me he had no face I didn't believe her."

"Louise?" the sheriff asked.

"That's my daughter," Mother said. "Louise is her real name. Gypsy is a stage name, a burlesque stage name."

The sheriff nodded in sympathy at Mother's inflection of the word burlesque.

"I cried for days when she first went into that awful theater

. . ." Mother started crying again at the very thought of it. She leaned her head on the sheriff's chest and let herself go.

Biff looked at me and winked. "While she was crying, though," he said, "she was eating, which was a damn sight more than when they were doing that broken-down vaudeville act of theirs."

The sheriff began to pat Mother's tousled head. Then he caught himself. With a quick glance to see if we had been watching him, he pulled his hand away.

"You're a brave little woman," he said to Mother. "Burying that body all by yourself. That took real courage."

Mother stopped sobbing. She brushed a fat tear from her cheek. "A mother's love, you know," she said. She swayed a little at that, and the sheriff put out his arm again. Mother naturally swayed right into it.

The sheriff had a look of deep concern on his face as he looked down at her.

"I'm afraid I'm getting a little faint," Mother whispered.

Biff looked from Gee Gee to me. We all knew what Mother could go through without getting faint.

"I think you should go back to the trailer," the sheriff said.

"No," Mother said with a great effort. "My duty is here, with my child," She braced herself and threw back her head bravely. With a quick, almost birdlike motion she reached for a square of white linen the sheriff held in his hand.

The sheriff wasn't birdlike but he was quicker. He put the handkerchief back into his pocket.

"I'm sorry," he said apologetically. "We found this in the grave, and it might be a clue. There may be a laundry mark or something on it."

He handed Mother his own handkerchief, and she dabbed at her dry eyes. Then she looked at him innocently.

"You mean you can tell things by laundry marks?" she asked. Her eyes were too wide and too innocent.

I would have given plenty to get a good look at that handkerchief. When Mother's eyes get that wide and that innocent, she is up to something. And when Mother is up to something, it's a cue to watch out.

The sheriff began telling her how important every detail was. "Especially in a murder case," he added slowly. "I know what you all have been through, and believe me I'd rather cut off my right arm than have to put all these questions to you, but I'm the sheriff and I just have to. This ain't like our regular murders. We always know right off the bat who kills who, why they do it, when they do it, and how they do it. We almost know *before* they do it. This is different. These two murdered men are strangers to me. You folks are strangers to me. I have to know everything."

"Why of course," Mother said. "What would you like to know first?"

"I'd like to know who this corpse is."

We all stared down at the dead man at our feet. Gee Gee turned her head away first. A gurgling noise came from her throat.

"You know him?" the sheriff asked quickly.

Gee Gee shook her head wildly. Her teeth chattered. "No-no," she said.

Mother moved toward her calmly. "You've been drinking too much," she said in a motherly tone. "That's what makes you shake so." She reached into her pocket for a handkerchief and handed it to Gee Gee.

Then she turned around and smiled at me. Her eyes were very blue. There wasn't a trace of worry in them. She glanced at the sheriff's back through the corner of her eye, then she winked at me.

Her mouth framed the words, "Leave it to me."

I tried to smile back, but it was too much for me. If I could only have some idea of what Mother planned on doing, I could feel more reassured, but Mother never knew herself until after she had started the ball rolling. By then it was always too late.

8 MOTHER WAS THE FIRST ONE TO HEAR THE TRUCK. "Listen!" she said.

We listened. There was a loud knocking. I knew the

bearings were burned out before I saw it. And after one quick glance I knew there was more than that wrong with the open-stake-body truck. Ysleta must have prided herself on the museum quality of her vehicles. First the sheriff's car, now this! It had once been painted green, an uncomfortable green. Lettering on the sides read: COAL-WOOD-ICE. The front door was held shut with a piece of rope. There were patches of adhesive tape running crisscross over the windshield. That, I decided, was to keep the thing from falling in the driver's lap. Instead of four mudguards, there was one. It was hanging noisily to the truck by the grace of a shred wire. The collector's item stopped in a cloud of dust within a few feet of us, and three men jumped down from the front seat.

I thought I recognized one of them until he came closer. Then I knew I had never seen him before, but I could tell by the black bag he carried that he was a doctor. He said hello to the sheriff. Then he walked over to the grave and looked down at the corpse.

"First one this year, eh, Hank?" he said to the sheriff.

He knelt down and opened the dead man's coat. The ragged tear in the lining caught his attention.

"Stranger," he said almost to himself.

"How long would you say he's been dead?" the sheriff asked.

"Hard to tell in this weather," the doctor replied. "Twenty-four hours maybe. I can tell better when I get him opened up."

Gee Gee let out a sickish gasp, and the doctor looked at her.

"You find him?" he asked.

"No." Mother replied placidly. "I found the body. It was in our bathtub."

"Not this one, Mother. It was the other one that was in our bathtub. Remember?"

The doctor raised one black eyebrow. He glanced at the sheriff questioningly.

"Actors," the sheriff said, as though that explained everything. "Living in a trailer at Restful Grove. They knew the corpse in the first, in fact, this little woman here buried it."

Mother smiled as though she were taking bows at the Met. The smiles were wasted on the doctor.

He beckoned the two men who had arrived with him. They brought over a large piece of canvas and rolled the body up in it. They tossed the bundle into the back of the truck and climbed in next to it. The sheriff and the doctor got into the front seat.

"Drop me at the bend," the sheriff said to the doctor. "I'll pick up my car there. See you folks later," he added to Biff and me. With Mother it was a little different. "Get some rest, Mrs. Lee," he said. "When you feel better, maybe we'll have a little talk."

Mother waved sadly as the truck drove away. Then she turned to me.

"Well, that's over," she said in a businesslike tone. "I told you I'd fix everything, didn't I?"

The unbelievable part of it was that Mother really thought she had fixed everything. The bodies were out of our hands, and that is as far as Mother's mind could travel in one direction.

As we walked toward the trailer I asked Mother about the package.

"What package, Louise?" Mother said.

Biff and Gee Gee were walking ahead of us. I lowered my voice. The package was too small to be another body, but I still didn't like the way mother was evading the question.

"The package you put into your apron pocket," I whispered. "Where is it now?"

Mother stopped and stared at me. "Do you feel all right, Louise?" she asked. "I really think sometimes that you aren't as bright as you might be. Package? I never had a package."

In her own way Mother had convinced herself that she had nothing in her pocket when she walked toward the grave. There was nothing I could do about it. Nothing but pray, that is.

I prayed and Mother hummed.

She found seven four-leaf clovers on the way to the trailer. She was in a happy mood because of it. She kept humming too loudly for me to get a word in edgewise.

I wanted to ask her about the handkerchief; why she wanted

it. I wondered if the sheriff noticed she had one of her own when she asked him for his. I wondered what was in the package Mother had forgotten about. I wondered if there was a drink left in the bottle. Most of all, I wondered that. I wanted one or two, maybe three of four, and I wanted them right away.

Mamie had set the table, and the teakettle was singing away when we arrived at the trailer. Gee Gee left us at the door. She said she was going to rest for a while. Corny had taken up all the resting room as usual, but Mamie settled the situation nicely.

"Get up, you lazy lummox," she said.

I couldn't believe my ears. Neither could Biff. Corny not only got up; he left the trailer. With a blanket under his arm he stomped away to a hammock near the shower house.

Mamie was still mumbling when she joined us under the lean-to tent. "I won't take any of his lip, that I won't." She looked at Mother and her mood changed quickly. "You poor dear," she said sympathetically. "Here, let me fix you a nice cup of tea. It'll relax you."

Mother allowed herself to be placed in a camp chair. She smiled wanly at Mamie, who puttered around getting the can of milk and the sugar bowl.

"I couldn't help but hear Louise on the phone," Mamie said. "It must have been an awful shock. Just imagine a dead body in your own trailer. Well, I always say, you never know what's liable to happen next. The way the world is today . . ."

Mandy looked up from his *Racing Form*. "Well, one thing is sure. They can't blame that on Roosevelt."

"Can't blame what?" Biff asked sharply.

"Alabaster coming in last," Mady replied. "What didja think?"

Biff sighed deeply. So did I, for that matter. Sooner or later everyone would have to know about the corpse, but for the time being I was just as pleased to have it later. It was the sheriff's job to tell anyway, I reasoned.

Mandy got up to leave, and Biff gave him six dollars.

"Across the board on Black Night in the sixth at Rockingham," Biff said.

A trailerite was taking the bets. I think Mandy could have found a bookie in the Sahara desert. He waved to Mamie. "Wish me luck sweetheart," he said.

Mamie wore one of Mother's gingham dresses. As she moved about it flopped around her thin hips. Mother wore low necks because her throat was full and lovely. Mamie's neck needed something to cover it. The white organdy ruffle that looked so crisp and dainty on Mother was grotesque on poor Mrs. Smith.

Biff must have been thinking the same thing.

"When we go into town for groceries, you come with us, Mamie," he said. "We gotta get you some dresses. Can't have the ingénue of the layout going around in hand-me-downs."

Mamie turned her head away. I was sure she was crying.

"You're all so wonderful to me," she sobbed. She hurried into the trailer, and Biff drank his tea silently. After a moment he glanced up from the streaming cup.

"Hell's bells, I didn't mean to make her cry. I only . . ."

"I know, honey."

Mamie opened the screen door and called to Mother. Her voice was light and gay. "Dearie! Make some room on the table. I have a surprise for you."

Mother moved the tea things listlessly. She seemed to be thinking of something else, something that worried her. Even when Mamie placed the baking dish in front of her, Mother remained pensive. The dish was full of golden-brown biscuits.

Biff gave them a triple take.

"I thought they'd go good with the tea," Mamie said. "I had an awful time with the oven, though. Kept burning on the bottom." She lifted a biscuit and felt its weight, first in one hand, then the other. "I do hope they aren't heavy," she said.

It was the first time I knew we had an oven. Our meals had been sketchy. Beans, hamburgers, hot dogs, then back to beans again. We hadn't made a career of the eating business.

From the expression of Biff's face I decided there was something in that "The-way-to-a-man's-heart" dialogue. If biscuits would make his eyes sparkle like that, he was going to have biscuits if I had to make them myself.

When he was buttering his sixth, I noticed the line of laundry. On a rope stretched from the tent to a tree, four sheer nighties waved invitingly in the breeze. A pair of lacy panties, men's socks, my new nylons, and a pair of men's shorts, lavender ones.

Mamie, watching me, spoke quickly. "I did the dainty things first. Tomorrow I'm getting at the shirts and the heavy stuff."

My first reaction was of resentment. I didn't like having a stranger doing my laundry. Then I felt ashamed and grateful. I hate doing laundry myself.

Dimples's voice rose petulantly from the other trailer. She couldn't find her eyebrow tweezers. "They were right here on the stove," she said.

"You pull out one more hair," Gee Gee said, "and you'll be balder'n a bat."

Mamie rushed into the trailer. She closed the screen door carefully.

I put all the makeup things in this drawer," she said. "It'll take me a little while to learn what belongs to who, but . . ."

As her voice trailed off I felt Biff look at me.

"Did I call her an ingénue?" he said softly. "I shoulda called her the leading lady."

He was right. Instead of worrying how crowded we were, I was thinking how nice that our family was larger by one.

Biff ate the last biscuit carefully.

"This is what I call eating high off the hog," he said as he swallowed it in two bites.

Mother sipped her tea. She lit a cubeb and blew out the smoke in tight little gasps.

"You know," she said slowly, "I was just thinking." She took another puff from her asthma cigarette and let us worry for a moment. Mother's thinking could be troublesome at times.

"I didn't want to tell the sheriff until I spoke with you." The last was directed at Biff: "The way you keep getting things mixed up all the time. I don't feel that I should, well, trust you."

I knew then that whatever Mother had been thinking, it

wasn't good. I prepared myself for the worst, but her next words stunned me.

"I think that handkerchief the sheriff had in the hat was Cliff's."

Biff gulped.

"I saw the laundry mark," Mother said. "I remember it from when we sent out that bundle in San Diego. Remember how I happened to send it out marked Lee by mistake?"

Hardly by mistake. I thought. Mother had just been protecting my billing. Even on the laundry lists I had to headline. At the time we thought it was amusing when the dry cleaning and the laundry were all marked Mr. G. R. Lee. When the neighbors began calling Biff Mr. Lee, we stopped laughing.

"There was something else, too," Mother said.

Biff leaned back in his chair and took a deep breath. I tried to brace myself, too, but that old feeling tightened across my chest.

"But," Mother added mysteriously, "because of your big mouth I'm not going to tell you what it is." She leaned over her teacup and stared at the matted leaves.

"Gypsy," she said.

I knew that was coming. When Mother called me Gypsy she either wanted me to lay out the cards or read the tea leaves. I was in no mood for making like a fortune-teller. I set my jaw firmly. I had every intention of saying no.

Mother poked around in her teacup with a pinky. "I think I see something interesting," she said.

I crossed my arms and leaned back in my chair.

"Of course, I can't read it," Mother said, "but it certainly looks like a gun to me."

In spite of my intentions I was dying to get at the cup. Ever since I had predicted the death of Lolita La Verne at the Old Opera Theater I was convinced I was the white-haired girl of the oracle racket.

"Well, if that isn't funny!" Mother chuckled her tongue against her teeth. "Just as plain as day I see the sheriff's hat, the way it goes up high in back and comes to a point, and everything. It's uncanny, that's what it is, uncanny."

"Like the hotel without any bathrooms," Biff mumbled.

I shot him a quick glance, and he went back to his tea.

Mother turned her cup upside down on the saucer. She spun the cup three times to the right, then three times to the left.

"Did you make a wish?" I asked.

Mother nodded. She was very serious as she handed me the cup.

I didn't see the sheriff's hat. I did see something that could be interpreted as a gun. That is, if they make a gun without a handle. The only guns I was acquainted with were the kind used in sharpshooter acts. The gun in the cup was quite different.

"I see a journey," I said. With my fortune-telling I usually start off with a journey. In show business you can't go wrong seeing a journey.

"There's a letter or a legal document, a tall man, and a—a marriage."

I looked up in the cup again. It was the first time I had seen a marriage in the tea leaves. Two straight lines side by side. I turned the cup around and looked again. No matter which way I read it, there was marriage in my mother's cup.

"A marriage?" Mother looked more serious than ever. "See if you can find any initials."

There was one letter near the edge. It was a large D. I didn't associate it with the marriage. It was too far from the two straight lines. I had an uncomfortable feeling that the letter D meant danger. I handed the cup back to mother and went into the trailer.

It took me a moment to get used to the gloom after the late-afternoon sunlight. The living room was empty. Mamie and Dimples were talking to Gee Gee in the bedroom. She sat on the foot of the bed, a Turkish towel around her shoulders. Her red hair was combed flat against her head.

"We're trying to tell her how good she'd look as a blonde," Mamie said. She stood, with the toothbrush in hand, ready for the first application of white henna. It was in a saucepan on the bed table.

"I done it plenty of times," Mamie said. "All my customers were pleased, too."

Gee Gee hesitated. 'I'd hurt my billings is all," she said thoughtfully. "Of course, we could change 'The Red-Haired Dynamo' to 'The Blonde Dynamo.' Or what ya think of 'The Blonde Bombshell'?"

Dimples sprawled out at the back of the bed, flicked her ashes indolently on the floor. "It's been done to death," she said.

Mamie listened with a happy grin on her face. She stirred the white henna and added soap flakes until it looked like a snowdrift.

"My, how I would love to see you girls act on stage," she said. "When I think you're all actors and actresses I get so excited. I don't know what I'm doing. Me, Mamie Smith, traveling with a show troupe! No one in Watova would ever believe it."

"Watova?" Dimples stared at her. "Where the hell is that? Europe?"

"Watova is where I was born," Mamie said with pride. "My dear husband, Mr. Smith, had a six-hundred-acre farm there. It's eight miles south of Oologah."

Dimples relaxed. "Now I know," she said.

"If I ever told them in Watova that I was traveling with a show troupe they'd never believe me."

"You said that once." Dimples was bored with Watova. She yawned loudly.

Mrs. Smith beamed on her. Yawn or no yawn, Dimples was an actress, and that was enough.

"I'll bet you're a big hit on the stage," Mamie said. "You must be beautiful when you're dressed up."

Dimples narrowed her eyes. "Are you trying to kid some-body?" she asked.

Mamie went on gaily. "Don't you ever get embarrassed tak-ing off your clothes with all those men looking at you?"

"Say." Dimples put her hands on her fat hips. "Where do you

get that embarrassed business? Why should I get embarrassed? I got a dark blue spot on me all the time ain't I?"

Mamie realized she had touched a sore spot with the Queen of Quiver. She tried to cover it up quickly. "I only mean, what do you think about when you're out there—taking off your dress like?"

"I ain't thinking anything," Dimples replied. "I got a job to do. I let the jerks do the thinking. That's what they paid their dough for. I'd look cute out there, thinking." She laughed briefly. "Boy, that's rich! Me, with a rhinestone in my navel, thinking!"

Gee Gee had enough of Dimples on the subject of Dimples.

"Hey," she said. "We were talking about me. Should I dye or shouldn't I dye?"

I had completely forgotten the corpse and the handkerchief and the package. At that moment Gee Gee's decision seemed more important. She had built up a reputation as "The Red-Haired Dynamo." To change it at this late date was something that needed consideration.

Dimples snatched the toothbrush from Mamie's hand and in one quick motion dipped it into the white henna and spread in on Gee Gee's head.

"When in doubt, act," she said. It was the motto Dimples lived by.

Mamie left the henna pack on a little too long. Gee Gee emerged as a platinum blonde. Platinum with touches of pink here and there to relieve the monotony.

Mamie was delighted with her handiwork, but I was glad that Gee Gee didn't plan on working for a few weeks. Even with her new title, "Platinum Panic," she'd have a hard time convincing the audience. I didn't have the heart to suggest that we dye her back to a redhead. I thought it could wait a few days. I did suggest that we needed a nip.

The boys were only too glad to join us. Corny got the glasses. That was the one job we could depend on him for. If someone paid for the bottle, he would always get the glasses. Mandy got the water chasers. He wasn't very cheerful. Neither was Biff. They had their my-horse-didn't-come-in look.

Biff eyeing Gee Gee's hair, was generous. "I could go for you myself," he said.

"Don't do me no favors," Gee Gee replied. "So far I'm the only dame in burlesque that isn't a sister-in-law of Gyp's. Let's keep it clean."

Biff, to change the subject, offered Mamie a drink. I was surprised when she took it. She polished it off like a seasoned trooper.

"Mmm, tasty," she said. She wiped her mouth with the back of her hand. "Not as sweet as my rhubarb wine, but tasty."

Biff urged her to have another. He didn't have to do much urging. Watova raised a breed of double-fisted drinkers, that was certain.

Mandy had gone into his specialty; imitations of birds and beasts of the forest. Mamie choked with laughter on her third drink as he did his version of a lonesome cow. The fact that a cow is hardly a beast of the forest didn't enter into the thing.

By the time Gee Gee went into her guitar solo, we had a pretty fair-sized audience. The neighbor trailerites kept a safe distance, but they were all there. Biff and Corny almost stopped the show with their scene, "Fluegal Street," and before we could stop her, Dimples went into her strip. The neighbors didn't know whether to applaud or to call the cops. One lone voice rang out, "Take it off!"

That was all Dimples needed. Biff had the courage to stop her. He grabbed Corny's blanket and put an end to the show. It was a fine party. We forgot to eat dinner. That is always a good way to tell.

Johnny's father let us borrow his car and in high spirits we left for the village.

"This will be one night we don't forget for a long time," Biff said as he helped Mother into the back seat. For once in his life, Biff was right.

9 WE MADE THE HAPPY HOUR OUR FIRST STOP. BIFF was driving, so that may have accounted for it. While he parked the car, Mother and I looked up and down the street.

It was very gay and colorful. The neon signs and the blinking lights reminded me of the Mulberry Street Festival. Most of the saloons had entrances that were more inviting than Fransisco Cullucio's, but, from the crowds hanging around the entrance, it was evident that he did the biggest business. The faded awning was half-raised. On it hung pennants with NOGALES printed on them and pillowcases with poetry addressed to MY SWEET-HEART stamped on the rayon satin.

I was surprised to see the number of wine parties in the saloon. The Happy Hour didn't have a beer crowd, even if they did look it. Most of the men were in their shirt sleeves. Many of them wore souvenir hats, Mexican sombreros with little balls hanging from the brims. All the women wore evening gowns.

Joyce Janice sat with four men at a table near the door. She still wore her sweat-stained blue satin. Cullucio stood within five feet of her. When we came in he nodded to us over his unlit cigar. He seemed rather surprised to see us.

We must have looked like a wine party to the headwaiter, because he cleared a table for us immediately. The table was too close to Joyce Janice to please me, but it was near the stage and Mother liked it. Mother never wants to miss anything.

"My Gawd!" Dimples squealed. She threw her arms around Joyce and began kissing her. "It's just like old home week. I just seen Milly and Clarissima at the bar. Bob Reed was there, too. This is wonderful."

From where I stood they looked like long-lost relatives. Shows what four men buying wine in a saloon can do. I think Dimples would throw her arms around a Gila monster if she thought she could get a bottle of wine from it.

Gee Gee was more restrained but just as anxious. With very little persuasion they both joined Joyce and her party of spenders. All four of the men were named Joe if Joyce's introduction counts. They were all from St. Louis and they were all out to have a good time.

"Well, so are we," Dimples murmured.

One of the men named Joe tied a napkin around her neck and placed a bottle in front of her.

"I'm not a baby, you know," she said with a look in her eye that made the announcement unnecessary.

I followed Mamie and Mother to the table. We had lost Corny and Mandy at the bar. They knew Milly and Clarissima, too. Bob Reed was a juvenile tenor from the Republic Theater in New York, and I had played the Gaiety with the two girls. They were bending an elbow and talking over old times.

If I had ever wondered what happened to burlesque when the license commissioner banned it, one look at The Happy Hour would have given me my answer. All the place needed was a couple of comics and a runaway. I'm glad the orchestra didn't play "Gypsy Sweetheart," or I would have gone into my number out of sheer habit.

With all the familiar atmosphere, there was something about the place I didn't like, something unhealthy.

"Well, what do ya want?" A pockmarked waiter in a dirty white coat stood at my back. His voice startled me into ordering a double rye.

I would have ordered it without being startled into it. I would have told him so, too, but he was too big for Biff to handle.

"I'll have a hot toddy," Mother said, "for my asthma."

Mamie couldn't make up her mind, so I ordered for her.

"Two double ryes," I said to the waiter's back. He was already on his way to the bar. Something about him lingered on. Maybe it was the general odor of the place. At any rate, I didn't like it. I didn't like the way Biff leaned over Joyce's shoulder, either.

"What in the world is Biff doing talking to that brassy blonde?" Mother asked.

"Probably just schmoozing," I said.

"Call it that if you like," Mother sniffed. "In my day we had another name for it."

The five-piece orchestra hit a sustained note and Bob Reed stepped out onto the stage, dragging a microphone behind him.

"Good evening, everybody," he said in his nasal voice. "Good evening."

The lights dimmed and a flickering spot picked him out of the smoke. He has never been exactly an ad for Scott's Emulsion, but now he was really letting himself go. His tuxedo was shiny and unpressed. Most of the shine was around the arms. From leaning on the bar, I knew. His face, without any makeup, was pasty white and pimply. Even his patent leather shoes were cracked and dusty. I blamed it on the climate; semitropical.

"It's good to see so many happy faces, so many familiar faces," he said. "Over here we have Nat Miller. Stand up and take a bow, Nat. You know, folks, Nat is a very bashful guy. He's in the liquor business. Come on, Nat, shake hands with one of your best customers."

Nat threw the master of ceremonies a cigar. It was all very chummy, I thought.

"And over here we have a wedding anniversary party." Bob pointed his cane to a group of people sitting in a far corner of the saloon. It was a relief to see a woman in a street dress. When the orchestra played "Many Happy Returns of the Day," she stood up and took a bow.

"Yes sir, Mr. and Mrs. Nolung," Bob announced. "Been married twenty-seven years and they couldn't get a lung."

The woman laughed and when Bob suggested that she get up on the floor, she not only obliged, but she did a little dance. Mamie thought it was wonderful until the woman showed her bloomers.

"And now, ladies and gentlemen, there will only be a short interlude before we begin the first half of our gigantic floor show. Mr. Francisco Cullucio, your host, has brought in a galaxy of stars for your amazement, I mean amusement. First, those beautiful girls, the sixteen lovelies, the Happy Hourettes. Then the dancing De Havens, straight from the Coconut Grove in Sedalia, Missouri. The French Sisters. Yesindeedy. Joyce Janice, the girl who thrilled millions with her dance of the swan. Turk and

Turk, the Turkish Delights. Your humble servant, Bob Reed, and, as an extra added attraction, the one and only, the queen of them all, Tessie, the Tassel Twirler! On with the show!"

As the lights went up there was a general stir in the saloon. From each table girls in evening dresses were hastily finishing their drinks to get to their feet. They all seemed to be saying the same thing: "As soon as the show's over I'll be right back."

The orchestra returned to their stands noisily. At a cue from the tired leader they played their last eight bars of "A Pretty Girl Is Like a Melody."

Almost swallowing the microphone, Bob Reed sang a verse and a chorus of the number. Then he announced the girls.

A tall, thin girl with bony knees was announced as Rio Rita. She paraded around the floor in a Spanish shawl. For a finish she let one side of the shawl drop and showed her bare thigh. It had a black-and-blue-mark on it.

They must be popular in Ysleta, I thought.

The second girl was Miss Whoopee. She wore cowboy chaps that ended where they usually do, but instead of wearing pants under them, she wore a row of beads. She was too busy chewing gum to smile at the audience, but it didn't matter. No one was looking at her face, anyway.

Milly, the chorus girl I knew, was wearing a tremendous shoulder piece of tarnished silver cloth. Paper orchids dangled from it. She worked hard to keep the thing balanced, but the effort was showing on her. Her smile was forced. She was Miss Kid Boots. I didn't recognize the character until I noticed the oilcloth spats that she wore over her dancing shoes.

Joyce was the last one on. I thought she was Miss America. She wore a red, white, and blue shoulder piece. Her G-string was one flittered star. She wore two smaller stars as a brassiere. She wasn't Miss America; she was Miss Ziegfeld Follies.

We got one more good look at the ensemble as they paraded to a chorus of "Lovely Lady." Just before the lights blacked out the girls took off their brassieres. It was a pretty dull opening.

Then the lights flashed on, Mother was slapping Mamie's

back. The bare breasts had evidently been too much for Mrs. Smith. Her face was a dull purple.

"Did—did you see what I saw?" she gasped.

Biff had joined us, and Mother glowered at him as though he had staged the number.

"Really, Biff, of all the *nice* places to go," she said, "you have to bring us *here*."

Two of the girls had shed their shoulder pieces and were back on for a snappy tap dance. Bob announced them as The French Sisters. The dance was more embarrassing to me than the nude finish of the opening, but Mother and Mamie applauded violently.

Turk and Turk turned out to be roller skaters. I've never cared much for roller skaters, so I took time off to look around the saloon.

Cullucio watched the show intently. He applauded first and laughed loudest when each act was finished. He was the only one who laughed at Bob Reed's quips. From time to time he glanced at Mamie.

She did seem out of place in our party. Her black straw hat with the one pink rose sitting defiantly on the battered brim was so incongruous. Mother's dress hanging on her thin frame was so obviously a borrowed dress. Even her leathery, wrinkled face stamped her as a misfit in our crowd.

Bob Reed started his act with, "On my way to the club tonight a very funny thing happened."

I didn't listen. There was a hat and a pair of shoulders near the bar that were altogether too familiar to me. I recognized the sheriff even before he turned around. He was talking to Mandy and Cliff. I nudged Biff.

"Well, that's nice," he said. "Think I oughta go over and maybe buy him a drink? And while I'm at it, sort of break it up?"

"Buy him two," I said. "And quick."

Bob Reed sang a parody of "I Want to Be in Tennessee." It was all about a little boy who puts his geography book in the seat of his trousers when he knows the teacher is going to whip him. With an eye on Biff and one on the stage, I suffered through the first part of it.

She started in. I began to grin.
When she pounded Alabam, Old Virginny she did slam,
Then she picked on Oregon.

Biff slapped the sheriff on the shoulder. I could almost hear him saying, "How are you, Hank old boy?" He had pushed his way between Corny and the sheriff. Little by little he edged Corny halfway down the bar. With a sigh of relief I turned back to watch the show.

The girls did three more numbers, and there was one more act before Tessie, the Tassel Twirler, made her appearance.

She was worth waiting for. I have seen tassel twirlers, but until I saw Tessie I never appreciated that branch of the arts. Tessie had talent. She didn't swing the tassels around any old way. She made them do tricks; one tassel going left, then the other tassel going right, both of them swinging right. Suddenly they began flying in opposite directions. She did tricks with her stomach, too.

I applauded as loudly as Cullucio. It was on the tip of my tongue to say how wonderful I thought she was when I saw Mamie's and Mother's faces. They were livid, I kept my comments to myself.

"Well, did you ever?" Mamie said.

Joyce followed Tessie. She did the same routine Biff and I caught at the rehearsal. She danced with all the gay abandon of a female wrestler. Her face was drawn and haggard looking. She was almost grim.

I didn't blame her. Tessie was a tough act to follow. It reminded me of how H.I. Moss, impresario of the Old Opera burlesque, used to take the temperament out of his most violent stars. He made them follow a strong act, too. The more I thought about it, the more I thought it looked like a put-up job.

Cullucio was standing at my side, one hand resting on our table. He chuckled softly to himself.

"She tells me she was a big star in burlesque," he said.

"She was," I replied. I knew then that I was right. Cullucio was learning show business fast. He had one of the tricks down, anyway. It didn't occur to me to ask what Joyce had done to incur disfavor, but he didn't wait to be asked.

"The boys don't think much of her around here," Cullucio said casually.

The rhinestone G-string made a pinging noise as it hit the tuba. I knew it was the end of the number without Mamie's gasp.

She jumped up from the table and with trembling fingers she tugged at the hat. The rose couldn't stand much more of the abuse she was giving it. She clutched the limp organdy ruffles around her neck and walked toward the door with the word ladies over it.

Mother picked up her pin-seal Boston bag and followed her.

"Whassa matter?" Cullucio asked. "They don't likea the show?"

"It isn't that," I lied glibly. "It's only that Mrs. Smith has never been in a saloon before."

"Saloon?" I call this a theater restaurant." His cold eyes settled on me. His teeth clamped down on the cigar.

I should have let it go at that. After all, he could call it the Stork Club for all I cared. To me, it would still be a saloon. I was uncomfortable with him standing at my arm, though. I didn't like being alone with him. I didn't like the smell of Caron's Sweet Pea and the stale cigar smoke that enveloped him. His white, belted suit was too tight, the black shirt too shiny.

To be sociable I smiled at him, but my heart wasn't in it. My drink gave me a little more courage.

"Saloon, theater restaurant. They're all the same to me," I said with a prop laugh. "I suppose what you've got upstairs you call a hotel? That crap table in the back room, that's strictly for ping-pong I guess."

I glanced at the bar to see if I could find Biff. He wasn't there. It gave me a deserted, desolate feeling. Where he had stood, there now sat three women. One of them—I learned later her name was Tanker Mary—was knitting. She didn't watch her knitting needles as she worked. Her eyes were on the door.

Every time a man walked in she smiled at him. Her lips framed suggestions that alternated with "Knit two, purl two." The other woman flashed two gold front teeth in a beery smile. "Want to have a good time, dearie?" was her standard remark. The third wore black cotton stockings on her fat legs, purple bedroom slippers on her feet. She was drinking beer; it left a white foam mustache on her mouth.

"That's a tasty trio you got there," I said to Cullucio. "Puts the customers in a happy frame of mind."

"What I care about their minds?" Cullucio asked. He drew out a chair and sat next to me. He adjusted his trousers carefully and he sat. He pulled them up to the top of his black-and-white buttoned shoes, flashing a pair of bright-yellow socks, brown legs, and purple garter.

I made a quick guess about his underwear. I had an idea it would be silk, with his name spelled out on the chest in contrasting colors.

"The Lucius Beebe of the border," I said softly.

A waiter passing by with a trayful of liquor stopped beside him.

"Want anything, chief?" he asked. The words came from the side of his mouth. His eyes were furtively casing me.

Too many Warner Brothers movies, I thought.

Cullucio waved him away. "If I did I'd ask for it, wouldn't I?"

The waiter smiled just like George Raft smiled in *Scarface*. "O.K O.K. Don't get sore. I only asked."

"He's pretty, too," I said as the waiter shuffled away. "Lots of savoir faire."

"New man," Cullucio snapped. "My regular waiter didn't show up."

"Well," I said, "you sure found yourself a good understudy."

Another waiter placed a check on the table. If he had piled the chairs on the table, he couldn't have asked me more clearly to get up and get out. He kept one anxious eye on the entrance of the saloon.

Customers were standing four deep waiting for tables. One

of them had slipped the waiter a fiver, I knew, for our table. Can't blame a waiter for trying to pick up a soft five, but even so, I didn't want him to think we were in the place as relatives of the boss.

"My husband will take care of the check," I said airily. I tried to give him the nod. The five-dollar-tip nod.

Cullucio snatched up the check. He pulled out a gold pen that must have weighed ten pounds and unscrewed the onyx top. With a flourish he scribbled his name of the check.

"My guests," he said to the waiter.

I cased the check. The amount hardly warranted such a display of generosity. It certainly didn't warrant the pressure of his knee against mine.

Biff's entrance at that moment was beautiful. In the grand manner of the old school, he handed the waiter a ten-dollar bill.

"We never drink cuffo," Biff said, "We pay. Then we can hiss the floor show if we want to."

The sheriff was with Biff. They arranged themselves comfortably in the chairs and ignored the boss of The Happy Hour.

"This joint sure does a helluva business," Biff said to no one in particular. "Yes sir, I'll take a pup out of this any day."

Cullucio leaned forward. I thought he was watching the dancers on the floor. Then I saw that his eyes were following Mother.

She and Mamie were returning from the ladies' room and Mother was smiling broadly. She had powdered her face and she looked lovely. The sheriff thought so, too. He almost knocked over my chair getting to his feet. Mother loved it. If anyone else flirted so openly with a man it would be inexcusable, but on Mother it looked good.

"This is my friend, Mrs. Smith," Mother said, pushing poor Mamie under the sheriff's chin. "It was her trailer that was burned up in that awful fire. She's moved in with us until she gets her insurance."

Mrs. Smith held out a limp hand and smiled demurely at the sheriff. She could have saved the personality. He hadn't taken his eyes from Mother.

Biff snapped his fingers at the waiter who was passing, the understudy waiter.

"Tequila for all of us," he said, "with beer chasers." Biff pronounced "tequila" with a hard double I.

"Make mine rye," I said to the waiter. Then to Biff: "You knock yourself out, dear. I'll drink what I can pronounce."

Biff hadn't heard me. He was waving his arms frantically.

Joyce, posed in the stage entrance, waved back. She had changed from her sweat-stained blue satin to a sweat-stained cerise velvet. I made a mental note about advising her to stay away from cerise. On some blondes it's becoming. Joyce wasn't one of those blondes.

In a moment she was at our table. She plunked herself into a chair next to Biff. It wasn't quite close enough to please her, so she wriggled around until the chair was almost in Biff's lap. She ignored Cullucio, who didn't seem to mind in the least.

"You left this in the ladies' room, dear," Joyce said to Mother.

She showed Mother a carelessly wrapped package. It was the same package I had seen Mother take from the trailer, the package I missed when we were standing beside the grave.

"Oh," Mother said as she reached for it, "it must have dropped from my bag."

Joyce leaned over and smiled sweetly at Mother.

"Could be," she said coyly. "Only I found it in the bottom of a towel hamper."

10

WITH ALL HER STRANGE MANEUVERS, EVERY now and then Mother does something that makes me proud of being her daughter. At that moment she came through with a quick one-two that made me feel like sticking out my chest so far that the local purity squad would have legitimate small beef. With no dialogue and a take-it-or-leave-it-boys gesture Mother snatched the package from Joyce.

"I wanted to show you this," she said to the sheriff as she unwrapped the package.

The sheriff, watching her, was almost as pleased as I. Joyce had been altogether too cute with her coyness, and the sheriff knew it.

I suddenly had a more comfortable feeling about the Ysleta police force. It wasn't Scotland Yard with all the gimmicks like fingerprinting and the business of having a guy named Lombroso who knows from faces if the suspect is a murderer or not, but it did recognize a good performance. And Mother, if I say so myself, was making like Duse. But I mean Duse in her prime.

"I bought it in Nogales yesterday," Mother was saying in an almost too-cultured tone. "You see, I sleep in the car alone. Sometimes I get frightened. I haven't wanted to alarm the children, but I have been followed. Oh, they don't believe me, but it's true. Since we arrived in this town two men have followed me constantly. I was a little nervous about it. Not that I'm a nervous woman, but these men are so—so—desperate-looking. Really evil. So when I passed the shop and saw this in the window I stopped in and bought it."

Mother uncovered a small gun. It was so small it looked like a toy. It had a pearl handle, and the business end couldn't have been more than an inch long.

Mother handed it to the sheriff. He accepted it awkwardly. I could understand that. The two engraved silver-handled guns hanging from a holster at his hips were large enough to arm a battleship. He bent the little gun in a way that made it appear as if it were broken.

Four tiny pellets rolled out into his hand. He examined the bullets, then the gun.

"Been fired twice," he said softly.

"Oh, I tried it out," Mother said. The Duse quality was out of her voice now. She was right back on Forty-Second Street, but still good.

"That's the way I am. Anything new, and I have to try it out right away."

Cullucio leaned over the table and looked at the gun.

"Hm, short twenty-two," he said. He smiled at the gun. Then he gave the teeth to the sheriff.

It was a waste of time. As far as the sheriff was concerned

there were two things that mattered. Mother came first; the fun was a slow second.

"Twenty-two?" Mother said brightly. "That's what the man told me. The man I bought it from. I told him I didn't want a gun that would kill a man; I only wanted to frighten them away. A little gun like this couldn't *really* kill a man, could it?"

The sheriff hesitated a moment. "Well," he said, "I don't know if it would kill him or not, but if you hit him in the right place it'd make him madder'n hell."

Joyce laughed boisterously. "That's terrific," she shouted. "I never knew you could be so funny, Hankie."

Biff came to the sheriff's rescue. "His first name is Hank," he said to Mother. "Everybody calls him Hankie."

I don't think Mother believed Biff.

Joyce had leaned over the sheriff's shoulder and was holding her glass to his lips. "Take a little drink," she coaxed. "Just us two. We'll make it a loving cup."

The sheriff was too busy rewrapping the gun to get the full benefit of Joyce's attitude. The cerise velvet was cut lower than the blue satin. The contrast of her heavily powdered chin against the bluish tinge of her neck was hardly attractive. But then, I might have been prejudiced. I really enjoyed the sheriff's unawareness of the private floor show. I liked the way he placed the gun in his pocket and patted it to see if it was safe. I like the way he looked at Mother when he asked if he could keep the gun for a while.

"It's a dangerous thing to have around," he said. "When you flash a gun you have to make sure it's better than the other guy's or you don't draw."

"I only bought it because I was nervous," Mother said softly. "Now that I know you are watching out for us, I don't need it anyway."

The sheriff turned as crimson as Joyce's dress. It might have been a reflection, though; she was close enough to cast one.

Then, with a broad, slow smile, she caught on. She let her tired eyes travel from Mother's flushed face to the sheriff's.

"Well," she said. "Looks like I missed the boat again."

The sheriff had the good grace to blush again, but Mother took the line in her stride.

"There aren't any boats around here," she said innocently. "We're inland."

I turned away to giggle and as I did I could see two men standing behind Mother's chair at the back of the room. They were whispering to each other. Mother caught my eye and turned around. The two men opened a door with a sign OFFICE over it and went into the other room.

"Those are the men!" Mother said. Her face was very white and she clutched the tablecloth in her tense hands. "Those men have been following me. They went into that room." Mother pointed to the door.

As she lifted her arm I could see how it shook.

Cullucio jumped to his feet. "In that room?" he asked. "Impossible! That's my private office." He pushed his way through the crowded saloon and, taking a key from his pocket, he unlocked the door of his office. He entered and closed the door behind him.

"Are you sure they are the same men?" the sheriff asked.

Mother didn't have time to answer. Cullucio had opened the door and was on the way back to our table. His dark face was wreathed in smiles.

"Nobody in there," he said casually. "You must have thought you saw someone. Maybe they went in that other door."

There was another door near his office, but I knew which one the men had entered. It was his office, all right, and they hadn't needed a key to get in. They hadn't knocked, either.

Biff was whispering to the sheriff. I knew he was whispering about Mother and her imagination. Mamie heard part of the conversation because she scowled at Biff and the smile she gave Mother was one of deep sympathy. I knew it was up to me to put the thing straight. I don't have Mother's imagination and I knew what I saw, but before I could speak I felt Biff's knee nudge me.

A telepathic thought came to me. Biff had his own reasons for wanting Mother to be disbelieved. In a flash I knew it. I kept silent.

Biff turned to Cullucio. "You got a great little show here," he said. "Strictly four-forty, but have you ever thought of putting in a couple comics?"

Cullucio leaned back in his chair and put his thumbs through his lucite suspenders. He was businessman enough to know when he was being sold a bill of goods.

"You talking about yourself?" he asked, half-smiling.

"How did you know I was a comic?" Biff asked. He was surprised but even more flattered.

"Certainly not from that short you made for Metro," I said.

"Matter of fact," Biff went on, "I was thinking about a couple of friends of mine. Solid comics. Good team, too. They worked together thirty-four weeks steady at the Republic in New York, sixteen weeks at the Rialto in Chicago, full season at the Steel Pier in Atlantic City. Records talk, and believe me those are tough houses to make good in." Biff looked at me. "Aren't they, Punkin?"

"Oh yes," I said, lying through my teeth. Of all the pushover audiences in the world, Biff had mentioned the three top ones. All a comic has to do is spit in his pants and he stops the show cold. "They really are a tough audience," I said.

Cullucio was impressed. He dropped his casual air and took his thumbs from his suspenders.

"I can't afford to pay much money," he said. "This business tonight, well, it's unusual."

Where, I thought, have I heard that before?

"I'd like to see them act, though," Cullucio said.

"See them *act*!" Biff was aghast. "You mean you want Cliff Corny Cobb and his partner, Mandy Hill, to give you an *audition*?"

"Well, I dunno . . ."

What Cullucio didn't know was the meaning of the word audition. That was obvious. Obvious to anyone but Biff, that is. Biff didn't give the man time to ponder, though.

"These are big-time comics, brother," he said. "The minute I saw your show I said to myself, 'What this place needs is a couple of comics, class comics.' Naturally, I think of the two top boys in the business. That is, since I got out of burlesque. I didn't mention it to them yet. I don't know how they'd feel about working in a saloon . . ."

"A theater restaurant," I said sharply.

Biff took the cue. "Want to talk business with them?" he asked Cullucio.

Cullucio lost his you-sell-me attitude.

"Sure I talk to 'em," he said eagerly.

Biff nearly upset the table in his rush to grab Mandy and Cliff while they still could talk. He brought them back with him to our table and introduced them to the saloon-keeping impresario.

Cullucio wasn't quite as eager after getting a good look at the pride of the Steel Pier.

"I'll see them in my office tomorrow," he said. He tossed his thumb toward the direction of the door with OFFICE printed above it. Under the OFFICE sign I saw another, OFFICIO. Cullucio wasn't taking any chances on having his sanctum mistaken for the men's room.

The two comics left to join the girls at the bar. Biff asked Mamie if she'd like to dance. When she said yes, he was sorry he had mentioned it, but he helped her to her feet as though she were the queen of the ball. Joyce left us to sit with her friends from St. Louis, and the sheriff danced with Mother. I was alone with Francisco Cullucio again.

"Maybe you like to work here, too," he said, after the surly waiter put two drinks on the table.

I took a good look at Cullucio and another at the waiter. No, I certainly didn't want to work at The Happy Hour. I didn't tell him that, though. I knew Biff had something up his sleeve or he wouldn't have acted as agent for Cliff and Mandy. I had seen Biff in action before. When he felt good and ready, he'd tell me his plans. Until then I was expected to follow through if it killed me.

"I'd love it," I said, "but I have a clause in my contract. No doubling. I mean I'm not allowed to hold down two jobs at once," I added hastily as I saw the bewildered expression on his face. "If you're looking for a stripper, though, I know someone who'd fill the bill."

I glanced over at Dimples and Gee Gee. I couldn't make up my mind which one to throw to the wolf. At a second glance I wondered if the wolf would sit still for either of them. Gee Gee's multicolored hair was scraggling over her freckled forehead. Her nose was shiny. She needed lipstick, I concentrated on Dimples. She looked worse, but Cullucio struck me as the type who went in for lushness, and Dimples certainly fit that description. The nickel a drink would net her a nice income, too, I thought.

"Her name is Dimples Darling," I said. "She's billed as the Queen of Quiver."

Cullucio's knee was pressing against mine again.

"If she's a friend of yours, I put her to work," he said meaningfully.

If the freighted glance and the pressed knee counted, it looked as though I was the one who was going to do the work. I only hoped that whatever Biff was doing was important enough to make up for what I was going through.

"Maybe we can make a deal with that contract of yours," Cullucio said. "I want you to be happy here."

"I know I would, Mr. Cullucio."

"Call me Frank."

"Frank," I gulped.

Mother and the sheriff returned to the table. The orchestra had gone into a conga, and they were both a little out of breath from dancing.

"Tomorrow, then, Evangie?" the sheriff whispered as he helped Mother into her chair.

"Tomorrow, Hank," Mother said.

The air was certainly full of June.

Hank took his hat from the chair and held it in his hands. "So long, folks," he said.

"See you tomorrow," Biff said from the dance floor. He hadn't heard Mother and the sheriff make their little date, so he didn't understand the sheriff's blush.

Mother picked up her purse and fumbled around for her asthma cigarettes. The conga had been too much for her, I knew. The instant she put it to her lips, Cullucio was on hand with a cigarette lighter. The lighter matched the pen, only it was even heavier and more ornate. Mother inhaled the pungent smoke. As she exhaled, her breathing became easier.

Cullucio leaned over the table and watched her intently. The overhead lights, reds and blues, made his hair shine like a rhododendron leaf that's just been sprayed with miscible oil. His face seemed darker, his teeth whiter. He dipped the end of his cigar in his liquor before he put it to his mouth, but he didn't light it. Instead, he suddenly got to his feet, turned on his heel, and left.

I watched the padded white shoulders as they traveled through the crowd. When they arrived at the door with OFFICE-OFFICIO written above it I lost sight of them.

"Well," Mother said, "if he isn't rude. You'd think he'd have said goodnight or something."

I was thinking too hard to answer her. I wondered what I had said to anger him. After all Biff's trouble trying to sell Cliff and Mandy, after my hours of playing knees, and after drinking that terrible liquor, I had to say something to spoil things! But what had I said? I couldn't for the life of me remember.

Biff and Mamie danced by the table. The rose on Mamie's hat was hanging down over her thin shoulder. As she bounced around with her own version of the conga, her dress flopped around grotesquely, but she looked as though she were having herself a time.

Mother's cubeb smoke was getting heavier. It was a sticky, sweet-smelling smoke like . . .

"Like Benny, the trumpet player," I said aloud.

"Who?" Mother asked politely.

"Nobody," I said. "Nobody at all."

The noise of the saloon was reaching a crescendo. The conga line raced madly around the small dance floor. I was dizzy from watching them, dizzy from remembering.

Without realizing what I was doing, I took the cubeb from Mother's fingers and ground it out in the ashtray. Mother looked at me as though I had gone mad.

"What in the world's the matter now?" she asked.

I couldn't tell her about Gee Gee and the marijuana. I couldn't tell her that her cubeb smelled exactly like a reefer. Suddenly I knew why Cullucio had been so rude. He thought Mother was smoking a marijuana!

"No wonder he was upset," I said. "He thought you were smoking a marijuana."

"A marinello?" Mother gasped. "Have you lost your sense?"

I shook my head. "No, Mother, I just had a flash. I think I know why Biff wants Cliff and Mandy to play The Happy Hour saloon. He wants an excuse to hang around."

"Biff doesn't need an excuse," Mother said haughtily, "not when there's a bar in the place." Mother put another cubeb to her lips and lit it. "I don't like this club at all," she said between puffs. "I don't like the manager, either. Trying to tell me I didn't know those two men."

"He didn't say that exactly," I said. "He just said they didn't go into his office."

"Whatever he said, I didn't like his attitude when he said it."

"Well," I said. "He isn't a beauty boy, but maybe he means well. If he puts Cliff and Mandy to work I'll be grateful to him, attitude or no attitude."

11 WE WERE AT THE DOOR MARKED OFFICE-officio at eleven-thirty the next morning. Corny, bleary eyed but determined, knocked. Dimples set her mouth in a big personality smile, and I braced myself for the meeting with Francisco Cullucio.

There was no answer.

A heavy odor of stale liquor and cigar smoke filled the dimly lit room. It hadn't been a pleasant odor the night before. In the morning it was worse. A strip of white sunlight from the open door splashed across the littered floor. The chairs were piled on the tables. The red-and-white tablecloths were stained and dirty.

"What d'ya want," an unfriendly voice asked from the back of the saloon.

"We had an appointment with Mr. Cullucio," Biff replied.

"He ain't here."

That was obvious, but Biff, being in a jovial mood, didn't mention it. Instead he opened the door wider.

The pockmarked waiter emerged from the shadows. He held a broom in his hand.

"Hey, close that door," he shouted. "Want the place full of customers before we can serve 'em?"

Biff closed the door. "Perhaps you know where . . ."

"He's at the store. Can't miss it. Name's The Emporium. Two blocks down the street." The waiter stood leaning on his broom. If Biff had been intending to question him further, the man's attitude discouraged it.

"Thanks," we said, almost in unison.

The waiter was right when he said we couldn't miss the Emporium. We could see the sign from the saloon: FRAN-CISCO CULLUCIO in letters a foot high, THE EMPORIUM in letters a bit smaller. A canvas banner stretched across the street. On it was written: PERFUMES. LINENS. FINE LIQUORS. CUT PRICES. A large, painted red hand pointed to the store.

Before entering we looked in the windows. Cullucio dealt in more than just linens, perfumes, and liquors, judging by the variety of articles displayed. Men's riding boots were shown beside English electric razors and German cameras. Chinese kimonos were folded with the golden dragons showing. Beside them were Japanese lacquer boxes. In the back were Hudson Bay blankets, bath towels, tablecloths.

Cullucio sat at a teakwood desk in the back of the store. He still wore the white suit, but he had changed his shirt to a bright-yellow silk. It made his face almost saffron. He scowled over a piece of paper he held in his hand.

Dimples and I stopped at a counter of Mexican novelties while Biff and the two comics walked over to the desk.

"Well, here we are, bright and early," Biff said.

Cullucio glanced at him, then went back to reading the letter.

"Sorry we had to leave before we got a chance to say good night," Biff went on, as though he had the man's complete attention. "It was because Evangie, that's Gyp's mother, got an asthma attack. We had to fill her full of that stinking medicine she smokes and it was makin' her sicker than the asthma."

I peeked at Cullucio from over a small fan with NOGALES printed on it. He had stopped reading. His eyes were still on the paper but they didn't move. I crossed my fingers for luck. Biff and I had sat up until daybreak trying to figure out a story that would clear us with Cullucio. When I told Biff about the cubeb, he nodded as though he knew all about it.

"Why do you think I was trying to get the guys a job?" he asked me.

I told him about Cullucio offering me a job too. Biff said later that it didn't sound like a job for him; it sounded like a position.

Now he went on talking to Cullucio. "She's had asthma since she was a kid. Suffers awful from it. Asked me to tell you she was sorry she had to break up the party."

Cullucio put the paper in a little wire basket on his desk. He smiled at Biff.

"Hello, hello. Sit down." He indicated a leather chair near him. Then he picked up a corner of the letter. "People all the time trying to sell me something."

Biff nodded to Corny and Mandy. After the handshaking was over they settled down to business. Biff got Cullucio to up the money from thirty to forty a week each. Then he called to Dimples and me.

Dimples settled for forty, too, with tips. Biff bought a pair of Chinese slippers for Mother. Cullucio gave him a discount, and we left.

Once outside, we all sighed deeply. Biff and I for relief, the others because forty a week is forty a week.

"Let's get one beer before we go home," Dimples said.

Three hours later we arrived at the trailer.

I was feeling my beers. Rye makes me happy and wide awake; beer puts me to sleep. So does champagne, but that's beside the point. While Dimples went through the steamer trunk for her music and wardrobe, I stretched out on the bed in the bedroom. I felt as though Biff and I had accomplished something. The sheriff, thanks to Mother, was on our side. Cullucio was unsuspecting. Our friends were working, it looked as though things were going along nicely.

"Now that Corny has a job he can move to the hotel," I said. It had been in the back of my head all the time. Saying it aloud gave me assurance.

"Uh-huh," Dimples replied. She had a stack of music and photographs on the floor and was going through them slowly.

"Do you think I oughta open with "Blue Prelude" or my cigarette number?" she asked.

"Both," I said.

She put the scores to both numbers aside. Then she started rummaging through the trunk for her costumes: chiffons, crumpled and faded, shiny velvets, feathers, and rhinestones. She piled them in a heap next to the music. She selected three or four G-strings, several net brassieres and placed them with the wardrobe. Frayed satin shoes and a garter belt with limp lace were the end of the collection. Dimples never went in for an extensive wardrobe. She figured that no one was interested in what she had on. It was what she took off that counted.

After she rolled the things in a suitcase and left the trailer I dozed off. It was dark when I awakened. I must have slept for hours, but instead of jumping I lay still and quiet.

Something had startled me. I thought it was Rufus, the monkey. Then I heard him snoring. The dogs were with Mother, I knew. They were visiting. Dimples should be rehearsing; she was called at five. But there was someone in the trailer with me, someone in the front room.

I heard a stealthy footstep, the sound of a drawer being opened. I tried to keep my breathing even, as though I were still sleeping. Someone touched the door to the bedroom. When I went to sleep it had been open, but it was closed! My eyes were becoming accustomed to the darkness, and I saw the brass handle to the door move.

I called out softly, "Who is it?"

The brass handle fell into place.

I jumped up from the bed and threw open the door. I snapped the button for the light. Nothing happened. Someone had pulled the plug that connected with the electric outlet.

"Who is it?" My voice sounded hollow.

There was no answer. A warm breeze from the front of the room told me the door was open. I felt my way along in the darkness until my hands touched the kerosene lamp. With trembling fingers I lifted the glass hurricane globe and placed it to one side. I found a match and lit the lamp.

The room was empty. The door was open, as I suspected, but there was no one there. The screen door was also open. I looked outside. Flickering lights came from the surrounding trailer windows. Someone's radio was playing quietly. That was all.

I closed the screen door and looked around the room. Everything was in order. No, not everything. The door to the pantry was open. Before I closed it, I looked inside to see if things were disturbed. The half loaf of bread was untouched, the coffee can in its place. The sugar bowl, the tea, the soda crackers, Mother's supply of asthma powder; nothing was misplaced.

I sat on the daybed. My legs were still weak. I felt I had to sit and quickly. Had I dreamed it, I wondered.

"I didn't dream the screen door open," I said aloud. "I didn't dream the doorknob turning either."

A voice from outside spoke suddenly. "Well, you're up."

I couldn't place the voice or face at the screen door. I must have screamed. It all seems so silly now, but at that moment I was as frightened as I've been in my whole life. Frightened by my own mother!

"Why, Louise!" she said. "You're pale as a ghost." She opened the door and called the dogs into the trailer. She had a bundle under her arms and she tossed it on the stove.

While the dogs jumped around whining for their dinner, I told Mother about someone opening the drawer, leaving the screen door open, rummaging through the pantry. Mother cut up the dogs' meat with a pair of scissors and listened to me.

"It must be your imagination," she said when I had finished.

"But the lights," I said. "They wouldn't go on. When I pushed the light switch nothing happened."

"It isn't the first time someone has kicked the extension loose," Mother replied. She put the dogs' meat in separate little piles on a newspaper and watched them eat. Then she opened the bundle that was on the stove.

"The neighbors gave me these beautiful bones for the babies." Mother held up four rib bones. I didn't think they were beautiful, but the dogs did. The monkey was fed his seeds, the guinea pig his carrot. Mother sat back and relaxed.

"Do you know, Louise, I've been thinking," Mother said. Her pause didn't frighten me; she looked too serene. "I'm not sure that saloon is a good place for Dimples to work. That man who runs it, I don't trust him, dear."

I went over and put my arms around her. Her hair smelled so clean and fresh, like new-mown hay.

"Neither do I," I said. "But Dimples can handle herself and, well, there's a reason."

Mother looked up at me sharply.

"You and Biff aren't getting yourselves inveigled into anything, are you?" she asked.

"It's a little late for inveiglement," I replied. "And, anyway, Biff has a plan. He's going to . . ."

"He's going to what?" Mother asked. Her shoulders had become taut under my hands. I could hear her catch her breath in a tight gasp.

"He's going to charge them ten percent agent fees," I said. I tried to laugh. It was no go. I reached in the pantry for the bottle of rye instead.

"Have a hot toddy while I have an old-fash?" I asked.

Mother nodded, and I put on the water to boil. I was glad to have something to occupy my mind, something to make my head stop pounding so. Pounding with unanswerable questions. Why had Mother been so anxious to bury the body? Why hadn't she told me about buying the gun? Why hadn't she given it to the sheriff the day we were in the woods? Why had she waited until Joyce forced her into telling him about it? Why had she changed so in the last few weeks?

A familiar noise disturbed the silence. It was the loud knocking of a car that had burned out its bearings. The headlights cast a beam on the door of the trailer.

"Hey, come out and see what we got," Biff shouted.

"We're in the wood, coal, and ice business as of today," Dimples yelled happily.

I went to the door and opened it. Biff was driving a truck. Dimples sat in the front seat with him. In the back sat Corny and Mandy. It was an open-stake-bodied truck, the same truck they had carted the corpse away in.

"No!" I shouted. I ran down the steps and reached Biff's side as he jumped down from the seat. "Not *this* car, Biff!"

"It's the only thing in town we could rent," he explained, squeezing my arm gently. "Ain't it a beauty? Ten bucks a week."

"Well," I mumbled. "The price is right. Does it go?"

Mandy and Corny climbed down from the back. Mandy was limping painfully.

"Damn right it goes," he said. "Right back to the guy that rented it to us." He limped over to a chair under the lean-to tent and fell into it.

"We'll put a hammock back there for ya," Dimples said laughingly.

Corny was silent. He stepped into the trailer and closed the door loudly.

"What's eating him?" I asked.

Dimples and Mandy laughed.

"Biff told him to get out. Said as long as he had a job he could move the hell away," Dimples said. "So help me. Gyp, I think that's the reason Biff tried to get us all a job, so he'd get rid of us."

"Not you, Dimples," Biff said. "You're as welcome as the flowers in—say, where's everybody?" Biff asked suddenly.

He walked over to the trailer and peered in the window. "Hey, Evangie, we're home. Where's Mamie?"

Dimples chipped some ice and dumped it into a bowl. Then she got the glasses from the outside cabinet. "Soup's on!" she yelled as she placed them on the table.

"Mamie is visiting, I guess," I said. I spoke casually. Not casually enough, though.

"What's happened?" Biff said.

I told him. It didn't sound like much. Even less than when I told Mother.

"And that's all," I finished lamely. "All besides the pantry door being open. The catch on it isn't good, anyway, so maybe it . . ."

Biff hadn't waited for me to finish. In two strides he was up the steps and in the trailer. He pushed Corny aside roughly and made a beeline for the pantry. First he looked at the catch. It *was* loose. Then he began taking the groceries from the shelves and placing them on the stove top.

"What *is* all this?" Mother asked. "First Louise acts like an idiot, now you. I can't stand all this excitement. It's not only bad for my asthma, but I don't like it anyway. Corpses under your bed . . ."

"Corpses under . . ." Corny stopped in the middle of his packing and let out a long, low whistle. "So that's what it was you were carting off to the woods. Well now, isn't that just dandy. A corpse, eh? Anyone I know?"

"I wouldn't be a damned bit surprised," I said.

Biff sauntered over to Corny. He put his hands on his hips and looked down at the grinning comic.

"Now that you know, I can ask you a few questions," he said.

"You ain't goin' to ask me a thing, see? From now on I'm head man around here. That is, unless you'd like your friend, the sheriff, to know what's buried out in the woods. Any questions to be asked, I'm just the little boy to do the asking." Corny laughed up in Biff's face. "That'll look swell in the papers, too," Corny said. "It'll be the end of you and your Goddamned high-brow burlesque-queen wife."

Biff got him first. A very neat one-two right on the eye. When his head hit the day bed, Mother gave him a quick one for luck. I handled the other eye. But nicely.

We didn't bother explaining that the sheriff knew all about the body.

"I'll drive him into town," Mandy said. "One body under the bed is enough."

He picked up Corny's bag and booted the comic through the door. In a second I heard the loud knock of the truck and the swoosh of the tires in the dust.

Mother never looked happier. She downed her hot toddy in one gulp and threw her arms around Biff.

"You were wonderful!" she said.

Biff and I looked at each other. Biff shrugged his shoulders. I shrugged mine. Mandy's remark about the body under the bed had evidently escaped Mother's attention, but it hadn't escaped ours.

Dimples burst into the room.

"Hey, what's all this about bodies under my bed?" she demanded.

"Not your bed," Mother corrected her. "It was under the bed in the back room. In the bathtub."

Dimples's chin sagged. Her mouth fell open.

"Gawdamighty!" she gasped. "When I heard Corny talking I thought it was a gag!"

12 WHY DON'T PEOPLE TELL ME THESE THINGS?" Dimples said. "Here I am, my opening night in a saloon, with all my worries about breaking in a new orchestra, worrying about how I'm going to go over, worrying about a million things, and out of a clear blue sky I hear we got corpses under the bed."

"Corpse," Biff said patiently, "not corpses. And it isn't there now, so quit beefin'. If it had been up to me you would have known about it the minute I did. The sheriff wanted it kept quiet until he got a line on who the guy was. He didn't want anyone to know until . . ."

"Does he know now?" Dimples asked.

"Sort of," Biff replied. "The way they got it figured out, he's two guys. He's George, our best man, and he's Gus, a guy who sold perfume backstage at the Burbank."

"If he's the Gus I know," Dimples said, "I'm damned glad someone got him. Of all the cheap, lowdown, miserable sons of . . ."

"Easy on the dialogue," Gee Gee said. "They still don't know who killed him. People hear you talking they'll think maybe you did. It's not only Gus. They got another one, too."

"Another what?" Dimples asked.

"Another corpse. What did you think," Mother spoke sharply. She was getting annoyed with the conversation. "And please get off that bed, I just fixed it."

Dimples jumped up from the bed and smoothed the coverlet. She punched up the three pillows until they were fresh looking. Then she whirled around and faced Biff.

"Two of 'em?" she shrieked. "Under my bed, yet."

I thought she was going to faint. So did Biff. He reached out to catch her, but Dimples changed her mind. Fainting wouldn't solve the problem at the moment, and she seemed to realize it.

"What are we going to do about it?" she asked calmly.

Biff shrugged his shoulders. "It has nothing to do with us. From now on it's up to the police."

"I hope you'll remember that," Mother said to Biff. She was busily putting back the groceries. "Dragging everything out; then leaving it for someone else to put back. Butting in where you don't belong. You'll see . . ." Mother slammed the pantry door shut. "The first thing you know they'll be three-degreeing all of us all because of your big mouth. If you had only let well enough alone, let me handle it the way I wanted to. But no, you have to go and tell everything you know. Ruin all my good work, and for what?"

Biff put his arms around Mother and hugged her. "Come on, Evangie, smile. There won't be any third-degreeing while I'm around. Questions, sure. After all, the body *was* in our trailer. We *did* know who it was. We *did* sort of put ourselves out on a limb when we buried him."

"We?" Mother exclaimed. "I love the way you give yourself all the credit."

Dimples had been listening with her mouth wide open. She shook her head once or twice.

"That's all, brother," she said after Mother finished speaking. "I'm taking myself a hotel room. Egg crate, flea bag, any kind of hotel is better than this. Burying a corpse!" She kept shaking her head as though she couldn't believe it. She looked at Gee Gee. "Did you know about this?"

"Yep," Gee Gee said. "I was in on the ground floor."

Mamie banged on the screen door. "Will someone help me, please?"

Biff opened the door, and Mamie struggled in with an ironing board.

"I've been all over this camp trying to borrow an ironing board," she said as she propped it against the side of the trailer. "You'd think people would travel with one. I know I'm completely lost without an . . ."

"And what," Gee Gee asked, "do you want with an ironing board?"

"Why, I want to press Dimples's acting dresses," Mamie said quietly.

We didn't have an answer for that. The *acting dresses* was too much for us. I was glad that Mandy returned at that moment with the truck. The ride into town would be cool, I thought, and getting away from Restful Grove would be a relief, too.

Mamie, with her ironing board, iron, and a pressing pad, climbed into the back of the truck. Dimples, with her costumes over her arm, fell in beside her. Mother with her asthma powder, Biff with a bottle, and Mandy carrying his theater wardrobe sat in front. I sat in the back with the girls.

"What about Corny?" Dimples asked Mandy though the back window as we drove toward town. "Did he find a hotel?"

"Yeah," Mandy said. "Only you know him. He won't put out that buck a night when he can pile in with us for free. He'll be back."

"Over my dead body," I said. The minute the words were out I regretted them. Not that the sentiments weren't right; it was mentioning a dead body that made me feel uncomfortable. Especially mentioning it as my own.

"How was his eye?" I asked to change the subject.

"I put a hunk of steak on it for him," Mandy said. The head-lights of the truck were dim and flickering. Mandy peered through the dusty windshield and leaned forward as he drove.

"I left him at the sheriff's," Mandy said casually. "He had to shoot off his mouth, Corny, I mean, and I thought he might just as well go to the head man while he was doing it. I wouldn't be a damn bit surprised if Hank didn't throw him in the clink. Boy, it was a rich scene. There's Corny all set to make Hank's eyes pop, and Hank just sits there and listens quiet-like. Corny builds it up, holding the corpse for the blackout, and just when he gets to spring it, Hank gets in ahead of him.

"'And why didn't you tell me about this murder a day ago?' Hank asks him. Then Corny starts sweating. He can't answer that one and he knows it. Hank answers it for him. 'In Ysleta,' he says, 'we got a name for guys like you. Blackmailers, we call 'em.'"

"And what did Corny say to that?" Mother asked.

"What can he say?" Mandy exclaimed. "He blustered a bit, but Hank was too close to the truth for Corny to get much gumption on it."

"Well," Mamie said politely after everyone had finished talking. "I hope he shows up for the performance. I've been looking forward to seeing you all act."

"For forty bucks he'll show all right," Mandy said.

The back of the truck was built for coal, wood, ice. For humans, no. At least not living humans. I could just manage to crawl down from it when we arrived at The Happy Hour. I ached in every bone. Matter of fact, I think I found a few bones to ache in that I didn't know I had.

Dimples felt it, too, but Mamie hopped down like an acrobat. She was all for carrying the ironing board right through the front entrance of the saloon until Biff took it from her and explained there was a stage entrance.

Mandy and I walked over to the gaudy saloon entrance. We wanted to see the building. Cullucio had certainly splurged in his adjectives. According to him, his three new actors were "colossal, supersensational, terrific."

"Everything but talented." Mandy remarked.

Dimples's pictures were plastered all over the entrance. A huge easel held four more. The one where she held a white fox fur up in front of her was center. One in black lace with a backlight silhouetting the body was to the left. There was one large, smiling head. How that got mixed up with the nudes, I'll never know. Maybe Cullucio wanted the customers to know she had a head; I'm sure they wouldn't have guessed from looking at the others.

My favorite picture of her was also on the easel. It was one Dimples had made years ago, but somehow she hadn't changed much. She was peeking from around a screen, showing just the side of her body. A suggestion of a garter belt, black lacy hose, and a bare breast. Someone had drawn a mustache on Dimples's mouth. She was billed, I noticed, as an Earl Carroll beauty.

"Caroll'll get the shock of his life when he finds that out," Mandy said.

He and Corny were billed as "Cobb and Hill. Those Two Funny Fellows. Songs, Dances, and Witty Sayings."

"That's done it," I said. "I'm going around the back way. Passing that billing is worse than passing a picket line."

Mandy took one last fond look. Then he followed me.

Finding the stage entrance was easy. We just followed an odor of dishwater, sour floor mops, and slightly spoiled food. The door was between two large garbage cans. It entered into a kitchen. The cook didn't look up as we hurried past him. I was just as pleased. I have seen cooks before, but this one had enough bacteria on his apron to wipe out the Japanese army.

The dressing room was to the right and opened into a long, narrow room that had once been a hallway, judging from the dimensions. It was directly behind the stage, and if the actors wanted to get from one side of the stage to the other, they had to walk through. The wardrobe hung on nails along the back wall. That left a space of two feet between the wall and the makeup shelf. None of the girls were in yet.

"What about my dressing room?" Mandy asked.

I couldn't tell him. I had a hunch there wasn't any, but he could find that out for himself.

"Ask Cullucio," I said, and Mandy left with a look of determination of his face.

The girls had made a clearing on the shelf for Dimples. The six inches of shelf allotted to her was at the far end of the room. The door opened in, and Dimples would have to get up from her chair each time anyone wanted in or out.

"They certainly aren't knocking themselves out being sociable," Dimples said. "I'd be more comfortable in the ladies' room."

I helped her unwrap her costumes and makeup, while Mamie plugged in the iron. Biff had set up the ironing board, and Mamie was puttering about nervously. Mother was having herself a time reading the different postcards and letters the chorus girls had been stupid enough to leave in the dressing room. She was very quick about it and I noticed that she hadn't lost the knack for placing the things back just as they were before. Mother prided herself on that.

Gee Gee sat in front of one of the mirrors and put on a full makeup, even to a blue eye shadow and heavy cosmetic on her lashes.

"It seems years since I made up," she remarked. Her voice sounded a little homesick.

As crowded and uncomfortable as the room was, there was a smell of theater about it, a smell that made me homesick, too. I watched Dimples as she began putting on her body paint. Even at forty a week I rather envied her.

"Gimme the sponge," I said. "I'll do your back."

Dimples used a flat-white body paint. It looked well in a blue spotlight, but in the harsh light of the dressing room it made her flesh look dead. She rouged the nipples of her breasts while I smoothed the white liquid on her back.

"Opening nights always terrify me," Dimples said. "I'm as nervous as a cat. First time in a night club and everything. The stage is so small, and instead of it going longways, it goes up and down. I'll feel so silly doing my number up and down. And having the audience so close to me."

"Close?" Gee Gee said. "Say, if they wanted to, they could reach out and touch you!"

"Omigawd!" Dimples said angrily. "You coulda gone all day without reminding me of *that*!"

Mamie finished the pressing. She gazed proudly at the fresh-looking costumes as she hung them near Dimples's place. She put the hot iron under the shelf and refolded the ironing board. She was almost as nervous as Dimples. Her hands were actually trembling as she fumbled at the doorknob.

"Come along," she said to Mother and Gee Gee. "We don't want to miss the first part."

Dimples closed the door behind them. She leaned her back against it for a moment before she spoke.

"You know Gyp," she said slowly. "There's something about that Mamie that gets me. It's the way she looks at me. Like I was a—well—a tramp or something. Then the next minute she knocks herself out doing favors for me. I don't like it."

"Maybe she's awed," I suggested.

"What's awed?" Dimples narrowed her eyes as she asked.

"I mean maybe the thought of all of us being actors has sort of thrown her."

My explanation soothed the Queen of Quiver. She sat heavily in the chair and began blending her whitish grease paint. I knew Dimples, but if I hadn't I would have formed a few choice opinions of her myself, especially as she sat there at the makeup shelf.

Her stomach was relaxed and it fell into three flabby folds. Her wiry yellow hair was curled tightly around her full face. The center part was growing in darker, and Dimples patted it gingerly with her powder puff. The dead-white body with the rouged breasts and the powdered hair did make her seem unusual. That is, if you didn't know her.

"Well," I said. "You can redeem yourself tonight. What number are you opening with?"

"'Have a Smoke on Me,'" Dimples said brightly. "I think the place is ripe for an audience number, don't you?"

The room began filling with tired-looking chorus girls. They weren't very sociable. Without a word to Dimples or to me, they settled themselves before their shelves and started making up. Even Millie and Clarissima were silent. After a moment I realized it wasn't rudeness so much as dullness. They just weren't awake yet. I was in the way, so I squeezed past the yawning girls and, after whispering "Good luck" to Dimples, I went out front.

In the main room I noticed that some of the early customers were taking their lives in their hands and eating the Chef's Special, a steak sandwich with limp French fries. On the side, for decorative purposes only, was one leaf of lettuce with a slice of soggy tomato. I couldn't watch the customers eat. Not with that picture of the chef's apron still in my mind.

Through the smoky haze I saw Mother and Mamie. They were sitting near the cloakroom very much as though they were sitting in the first row of the Roxy Theater. Mother's eyes traveled leisurely around the room. To anyone else it would have appeared as though she was quite disinterested. I knew better. I knew Mother was counting the house.

Gee Gee and Biff were at the bar. I joined them.

"Well, how goes it?" Biff asked me as I pulled up a stool and settled into it.

"If you mean the dressing room," I said, "it's intimate."

Mandy appeared from the crowd and sat next to me.

"Well, dressing room or no dressing room, it's for me," he said. "This gag of doing only two shows a night and having a bar so handy. It's a racket. Me, what's four a day since I got in the business and here I am with bankers' hours already. It's like stealing the dough."

We had one round on that. Then Joyce came in. No stage doors for the prima donna, I noticed. She made her entrance with the carriage trade, right through the front door. Naturally Biff asked her to join us and naturally she did. The bartender handed Biff the check.

Joyce drained her glass. Then she said, "That goes on mine."

The bartender smiled. "The hell it does, girlie. They was drinking before you came in. You'd chisel your own grand-mother, so help me, you would."

Joyce laughed softly.

"Well, can't blame a girl for trying," she said. "See you all later and thanks for the drink." She gave Biff a long, slow smile.

It was supposed to suggest a thousand intimate moments, but Biff wasn't having any. His rye with a beer chaser was more important.

Joyce sauntered through the room. As she passed the door with OFFICE-OFFICIO written above it, she stopped and tapped gently. There was no response. She tried the knob. It wouldn't open. Joyce started backstage. She walked slowly, letting her full hips sway from side to side. As she passed each table she paused for an instant. The customers were too sober to want company. Most of them didn't bother to look at her. I knew that once she got into her blue satin or cerise velvet it would be eas-ily sailing, but until then she'd drink alone.

The bartender was busy polishing glasses. He saw me watch-ing Joyce.

"She's a damn-good mixer," he said. "Makes more dough than all the other dames put together." There was a note of respect in his voice. "But is she a chiseler! If those other dames knew how she works 'em, the fur would sure fly." He hadn't dropped the respectful tone. If anything, it was more pronounced. "Yes, sir, she sure knows her way around."

Biff ordered another round, and the bartender kept talking while he poured the drinks.

"First night she's here," he said, "she comes up to me and offers me a proposition. The boss don't allow no downs here, you know . . ."

"Downs?" Gee Gee asked.

The bartender gave her a sharp look.

"Are you kidding?" he asked. "Downs is when you give the girls just enough liquor in it to fool the guy that's paying. Cullucio don't like that, he thinks it's cheating. I don't know what's better, cheating a little or having the dames fall down drunk in the last show, but he's the boss. Anyway, the first night, Joyce comes up to me and this is what she sets up. For every guy I toss her way she'll give me a fifty-fifty cut. Me? Well, I like to pick up an honest buck here and there, so I say sure. I let her chisel her way into plenty, even stick up for her when she gets into a jam with Tanker Mary. Well, sir, at the end of the week I look for my cut. Nothing happens. I ask her about it, and she slips me two bucks. Two bucks! I send her more than that in one night alone. So I just shut down on the little lady. I don't send her one customer, and what do you think she does?"

The bartender waited for Biff to say, "What?"

"Well, sir, she goes to Cullucio and tell him I'm watering down the stock. Me! The respect I got for liquor I should go watering it!"

Biff nodded sympathetically. He could understand that kind of respect.

"Maybe she was trying to get in good with the boss," Biff suggested.

The bartender poured another round.

"This is on me," he said. "If she was, she sure played it wrong. The boss don't like liars and from the way he watches us guys back of this bar, he knows damn well she's lying. Nope, he's a hot-and-cold guy, that Cullucio. Got funny ideas about honor and honesty. He can change in five minutes from the sweetest guy in town to the toughest. Just let him catch you in one lie or one fast deal and, believe me, you're out."

Well, I thought, that accounts for Tessie having the good spot in the show. Cullucio had gone into his little hot-and-cold act with Joyce Janice and there was the reason. I tried to dig up a sympathetic feeling for Joyce, but my mind wasn't on it. I decided to tell Dimples to play straight, at least until she learned her way around.

Two tired-looking women stood in the doorway. They both wore enough makeup to face an audience. One of them swung a red patent leather purse, the other sauntered up to the bar. Before she could seat herself, the bartender hurried toward them.

"Gowan, beat it, you bums!" he said loudly.

The woman with the red purse swore. The words weren't new to me, but she did put a twist on her swearing. If the bartender could do what she suggested, he would have a good vaudeville act.

"And button yer lip," he shouted, "or I'll kick ya out on yer ear."

He waited menacingly until the two women left. Then he came back to where we were sitting.

"If I wasn't firm," he said, "this place would be so full of whores the customers couldn't get in."

Biff coughed noisily, and the bartender got the hint.

"I mean it'd be so full of streetwalkers that it'd be awful."

Any feeling of homesickness for the theater I might have had was slowly disappearing. There was something unhealthy about The Happy Hour. It wasn't only the cook's apron and the surly waiter. It was more than the hot-and-cold Cullucio. Even the friendliness of the bartender made me uneasy. It wasn't the sordidness. After all, I've been in show business all my life; I know sordidness. Trouping with tab shows, carnivals, and vaudeville, a girl learns to appreciate the full meaning of that word. Then, too, burlesque is no revival meeting.

But this was different. This was something that made me feel like hitching the trailer to the car and getting as far away from Ysleta as the eight wheels would carry us.

13 WHEN THE SHOW STARTED, BIFF BRIBED ONE of the waiters to get us a table. They all knew us by then, and bribery was the only thing that would get us out of the barroom.

The show was routined the same as the night before. Dimples followed Turk and Turk, the roller skaters. Bob Reed introduced her as "Stageland's Loveliest." The orchestra played the introduction to her music, the lights dimmed, and Dimples made her entrance.

She didn't try to sing her number; she talked it. Her voice is thin and weak, but the customers usually hear enough. I couldn't hear one word of the verse that night. It didn't matter; she looked well. She wore her red chiffon trimmed with ostrich feathers. With it she wore an ostrich feather cape and a red satin picture hat.

Cullucio had given her a good spot in the show, following two men and doing the first strip number. He was watching her intently. When he saw me looking at him, he made a circle with his thumb and first finger. He held them up for me to see.

I nodded back. Then I nudged Biff.

"Dimples is in," I said. "The boss just gave me the high sign. All we have to do now is keep our fingers crossed for Mandy and your friend."

Dimples finished the verse of her number and went into the chorus:

Have a smoke on me,
Everyone is free.

She took a package of cigarettes from the bodice of her dress and tossed one to a man in the audience. The cigarette fell on the table and the man let it lay there.

Cigarette for you to try,
Chesterfields, they satisfy,
Or would you walk a mile for a Camel,
It's worth a while.

Dimples paraded around the stage, handing cigarettes to the men at the tables. They were beginning to catch on now, and as she came near them the more venturesome ones would reach out for her.

Here's an Old Gold to cure your cold.
There's not a cough in a whole carload.
And down from old Virginia
Piedmonts are sure to win ya.

Dimples stopped in front of a bald-headed man. She let out a little squeal of delight.

"Isn't he beautiful?"

She placed a cigarette in the man's mouth and lit it for him. He had a few hairs growing along the sides of his head. These few hairs she curled with her finger. She took a red ribbon from her wrist and tied it in a bow around one of the locks.

. . . With a Turkish blend we have Fatimas, too.

Dimples leaned over and kissed the man on his bald head. With a quick little run she was at the stage exit. She unloosed the feather cape and removed her hat.

Now don't forget the name of the cigarette that I gave you."

Just before she exited, Dimples flashed one bare breast. The audience was not trained to applaud for strip numbers. There was only a scattered round until Biff began. He cupped his hands to make the clapping sound louder. He shouted, "Take it off!" and suddenly the audience picked it up.

The orchestra played "Smoke Gets in Your Eyes," and Dimples was back on for her first encore. By then the din and shouting in the saloon reminded me of the balcony of boys at the Gaiety.

Dimples went into her bumps and grinds. She had slowed down a little in the past few years, but she was still the fastest bumper Ysleta had seen. Toward the end of the chorus she turned her back to the audience, removed her skirt, and did her quiver. The beads on her net pants sparkled like diamonds as she shook them. Dimples had originated the quiver and she still did it better than any other woman in burlesque. The beads began to fly madly as the orchestra played faster and faster.

"Tessie is going to find this tough to follow," I said to Biff. I was a little pleased. Tessie wasn't my friend, Dimples was.

With a quick movement, she pulled off her beaded pants. She stood in the blue spotlight just long enough to let the customers know she didn't get the name Dimples for nothing. Then she darted offstage. She had to do encore after encore before they would let her leave. It was a solid show stop.

"I'll be back in a minute," I said to Biff when the number was over. "I want to go backstage and tell her how swell it went over."

I hurried through the alley until I came to the familiar garbage cans. Dimples was standing in the doorway cooling off. Little drops of perspiration clung to her upper lip. Her yellow hair was damp around her forehead.

"It was great," I said. Then I saw the busboys.

There were three of them staring at Dimples in openmouthed admiration. I threw the skirt of her costume around her shoulders.

"You're not in a theater now," I said. "These guys aren't like stageheads."

Dimples clutched the skirt tightly as we walked through the kitchen. The chef still hadn't looked up. I began to wonder if he had made someone a rash promise. The chorus girls were dressed for their next number. They stood near the huge sinks that were piled high with dirty dishes. They still looked tired.

"What's with the cold reception committee?" I asked when we were in the dressing room.

Dimples shrugged her naked white shoulders.

"Search me," she said.

There was nothing to search unless you pulled off the adhesive plaster to see who won the turkey, but I let it pass.

Tessie said hello as coolly as the others. Then she turned to Dimples.

"Cover it up dearie," she said. "This place is just about as private as Grand Central Station."

The words weren't out of her mouth before the door was thrown open and Cullucio had walked in. Dimples grabbed a makeup towel and held it up in front of herself.

"Why the hell don't you knock?" Dimples exclaimed irritably. Then she recognized him. "Oh," she said, "I didn't know it was you. Well, how'd it go?"

"Good, good," Cullucio said. "Only why don't you let 'em see a little more? You leave too soon."

"Don't encourage her," Tessie said. "She'll be out there all night. That is, until the cops raid the place."

Dimples looked at her languidly. "I don't know about that," she said with a superior smile. "If you haven't got the place pinched yet, it's a cinch that I won't."

The dialogue had become altogether too familiar. Before I got in the discussion myself, I decided to leave. Unfortunately, Cullucio had the same idea. I was in no mood to walk arm in arm with him through the dark alley. He looked too much like the type who knows all about alleys. He might have been the one they had in mind when they wrote the signs, COMMIT NO NUISANCE.

"I think I'll go through the house," I said, "May I?"

"Sure," Cullucio said. "I'll go with you." At the door he turned to Dimples. "When you get dressed, come out. I want you to meet some nice people. Lots of money, and they like to give it away to pretty girls."

"Well," Tessie said, smiling up at Dimples, "that leaves you out, dear."

Bob Reed was on as Cullucio and I passed through the small

door behind the bandstand. Mandy and Corny were standing ready to go on.

Mandy wore a sponge nose. It rather surprised me. He always worked clean in burlesque and here he was on his nightclub debut in baggy pants and a spongy nose. The suit was really a street suit, but when Mandy bought his clothes he always liked to get his money's worth. Instead of buying a suit that fit him, he'd get one several sizes too large. Then he had the extra material. In case of fire, flood, or riot, as he would say. His red tie was six feet long and he wore a very small brown derby. His bushy hair held the derby straight on his head.

Cullucio took one look at him and howled.

"That's the kind of comedian I like," he said. "A classy comedian."

Mandy winked at me. I winked back. Mandy knew what he was doing all right. If that was Cullucio's idea of class, Mandy was just the boy to deliver the groceries.

I couldn't say as much for Corny. It might have been his surly expression that made him look more like a straight man than a comic. His eye was all right, though; a little dark, but Corny had covered it pretty well with grease paint. Corny was quite adept at covering black eyes. Of course, he'd had a lot of practice.

"Say, we don't have to follow that, do we?" Corny indicated Bob Reed's figure on the dance floor. "After all, he's out there doing our best gags already. Aren't we going to get any consideration around—"

Cullucio interrupted him. "A girl number goes first. Don't worry, I'm not so new in this show business that I don't know what I'm doing."

Cullucio held my arm and led me through the saloon. As we passed Mother's table Cullucio greeted her warmly. He might have said hello to Mamie, but her attitude discouraged it.

She was toying with a beer and, from the stiffness of her back, I had an idea that this was her last trip to The Happy Hour. She had disapproved so strongly of Tessie and her tassel twirling, and Tessie was an ice-cream-social entertainer in comparison to Dimples.

Biff waved to me from the bar, so I dropped Cullucio at his office.

Biff was sitting alone. I was glad of that. It was the first chance I'd had to talk with him in hours.

"Mandy is wearing a nose," I said, pulling out a stool and making myself comfortable.

"I told him to," Biff said. "Cullucio's idea of humor is having a dame take the seltzer water in the pants. None of the women would sit still for it, so I figured we'd settle for a putty nose."

"It's sponge," I said.

"Couldn't get any nose putty here in Ysleta," Biff replied. He said it as though that made Ysleta a very backward city. Almost as though he'd said there was no post office.

"You know, honey, I was just thinking," I said.

Biff glanced at me sharply.

"Did I sound like Mother?" I said laughingly. "Seriously, Biff, I was thinking. I'm glad everyone knows everything now. It's a load off my mind. All but one thing: did Gee Gee mention anything to you about Gus? About him being a fence, I mean, and a dope peddler?"

"Yeah," Biff said, "and I figure it's a good idea to let the sheriff in on it. He's liable to hear about it and he won't trust us if we don't spring it on him first. I got him pegged as a pretty solid citizen. I think he'd be our best bet. Tell him everything and we can't go wrong."

I was agreeing with Biff heartily when the swinging doors were thrown open and I saw Hank enter the saloon. He stood for an instant looking around the room, then his eyes settled on us.

"I was looking for you," he said. He didn't take off his hat. His manner seemed less cordial than usual.

"And where else would you expect to find me?" Biff said affably. "Where there's a bar you can always find me at it. Pull up a rock and make yourself comfortable." Biff yelled to the bartender. "One double rye for my friend!"

Reflected in the mirror by the bar was a white suit with padded shoulders. Cullucio's back was to us, but I knew he was listening.

The sheriff stared at the line of bottles on the bar shelves, or was he staring at the white shoulders, too?

Biff opened his mouth to speak. Then suddenly he stopped.

"We're on the Erie, eh?"

When Biff spoke, the white suit moved toward the office, but two men moved into the space Cullucio left. I'm not good at recognizing faces after my third rye, but I could have sworn they were the two men I had seen go into Cullucio's office.

Biff tossed a couple of bills on the bar. He pushed back his stool and helped me to my feet.

"Let's take a walk," he said.

"We'll walk over to my office," the sheriff said casually. Not casually enough to please me, though. It was almost midnight, and midnight is no time to get friendly with the police.

Not that Hank was being very friendly. The walk to the office was a silent one. It wasn't far, though, and the air smelled good after the staleness of the crowded saloon.

We walked past the entertainment district. Gradually the signs became smaller and farther apart. Then there were no more bars. The street had taken on the appearance of any small Western town. Neat little houses with white picket fences were side by side. They each had a patch of dry yellow lawn in front of them. Most of the houses were alike and they all needed paint.

At the corner was one house larger than the others. A battered car was parked in front of it. Next to the license plate was a green enamel plaque with a white cross on it.

"That's Doc Gonzales' house," the sheriff said.

As we walked by, I saw a strip of light shining through the worn window shade.

"He keeps late hours," I said, trying to make conversation.

The sheriff wasn't having any. He didn't answer me.

We walked on for another block. Then he turned into a walkway. I recognized the frame building before me. The sheriff's office was on the ground floor. A balcony ran around the second floor. The type of balcony they show in Western movies; just high enough from the ground for the hero to jump from it onto his horse's back.

The sheriff opened the door, and we entered his office. When he snapped on the light I was surprised at how different the place looked from the time Biff and I had been there before. The glare of the white overhead light made the room take on a businesslike appearance. When I had seen it before it had been flooded with sunlight. It hadn't looked like a sheriff's office. Now it did.

The sheriff seemed more like the law too. He arranged two chairs for Biff and me. Then he seated himself behind his roll-top desk. He opened a drawer at the right and placed a cardboard box on the desk. It looked like a shoe-box. He didn't open it right away. Instead he leaned forward on the desk and rested his weight on his elbows.

"I guess you know what's in that box," the sheriff said slowly.

Biff laughed. "Well I know it isn't a bottle or you'd have had it opened before this."

The sheriff didn't laugh with him. But he did open the box. He placed the tiny pearl-handled gun in front of Biff.

"That gun was purchased eight days ago in San Diego," he said slowly. His eyes were cold his mouth firm. "Not yesterday or the day before, as Mrs. Lee said, but eight days ago."

"You said that once," Biff replied. "We caught it. Only you don't know Evangie. A day, eight days, it makes no difference to her when she's telling a story."

The sheriff didn't take his eyes from Biff. They didn't even blink.

"It was bought in a pawnshop," the sheriff said. "For twelve dollars. It wasn't bought by Mrs. Lee. It was bought by Gee Gee Graham."

Biff's face fell into the stupidest expression. Maybe mine did, too. Only the sheriff's words didn't surprise me particularly. Had I been in Gee Gee's shoes *I* would have bought a gun.

I wouldn't have gone around shouting that it was mine, either, not with dead bodies scattered all over Restful Grove.

"She bought it under the name of Hazel Bronson," the sheriff said.

"That's her real name," I said. "Gee Gee Graham is a stage name."

"I know. I know quite a lot about the lady," the sheriff said. "I've had a complete report on all of you from the Los Angeles police. I know, for instance, that Miss Graham not only knew Gus Grange, but that she had reason to fear for her life at his hands."

"You probably won't believe this," Biff said, "but we were fixing to tell you all that as soon as we could get in touch with you. Another thing we had to mention was that Evangie thinks she recognized that handkerchief. She thinks it belongs to Corny Cobb. A lot of funny things have been going on lately, and I haven't been able to piece them together, but Gyp tells me someone was in the trailer. She was taking a nap and she heard someone prowling around. We know for a fact that this isn't the first time we've had company. There was that one time before when some guy slipped a corpse in our bathtub, too. Finding that handkerchief at the grave of the second corpse makes me absolutely certain that someone is trying to frame a member of our company. It's too coincidental that the handkerchief *fell* out of Corny's pocket. I think someone planted it there deliberately.

"As far as Gee Gee is concerned, you can talk to her yourself. If you think she had anything to do with it after she explains her connection with Gus, well, I'll put in with you. Mandy Hill is a jerk. I love him like a brother, but I got to admit he's a jerk. He would no more kill a guy than I would and I don't approve of murder. Especially when it's with knives in the back. We get enough of that in show business without bringing it into our private lives.

"Evangie is a changeable woman, but she's no murderer. Gyp here can't cut her own toenails because she's afraid of scissors. How do you think she'd be with a knife? Dimples, well, one look at her and you got your answer. Take my advice, you look for a guy who's been doing this sort of thing for a long time and you've got your man. This isn't an amateur's murder, and you know it. The guy who's responsible for those two corpses is a guy that's broken in his act and played it plenty."

The sheriff stood up. His expression certainly hadn't softened.

"I know you're all actors," he said. "If I didn't, I might pay a little attention to that talk of yours. Now, get this straight. I'm not arresting anybody, now yet anyway. You can't leave town, so don't try. I'm coming out to Restful Grove tomorrow and I'm questioning each and every one of you. One more lie, or one more evasion of the truth, and I lock you all up."

He opened the door for Biff and me. My legs felt a little weak, but I used them to get out of that office in a hurry. The sheriff closed the door behind us loudly. Biff and I kept walking. We didn't speak until we were halfway down the block.

"Of all the hypocrites!" Biff said. "And we thought he was fixed."

"Dancing with Mother like that," I said.

"Drinking my liquor," Biff said.

Then we laughed.

"Not only that, but he hinted that we might be *good* actors."

Ahead we could see the lights of the saloon district. The Oasis, The Blinking Pup, The Last Hole, finally The Happy Hour. We quickened our pace. The lights ahead seemed to make the street we were on even darker. It was too quiet, too peaceful.

The doctor's car was still parked in front of the house. The parking light threw a faintly red beam on the dried grass.

Suddenly Biff seized my arm.

"Listen!" he whispered.

There was a sound of a car starting up, the whir of a powerful motor. We stopped walking and listened closely. From one of the houses there was the click of a door lock falling in place. The beam of the headlights lit up and a low, cream-colored roadster sped down the driveway and into the street. It was headed toward the saloon district. It had left the doctor's driveway.

The strip of light that had been shining from under the doctor's window disappeared as Biff and I stared at the house.

"Did you get a look at the guy who was driving the car?" Biff asked.

It was Francisco Cullucio.

14 THE SHERIFF WAS AT THE TRAILER CAMP before we had finished our morning coffee. He had two men with him, the same men who had been with the doctor the day we dug up the body. They were in their shirt sleeves. The heat was oppressive, and their shirts were wet with sweat.

Instead of stopping at our trailer, they went directly to the one next door. Little Johnny's father opened the door, and the three men stepped inside.

Mother put her head closer to the saucer with the Life Everlasting burning in it. The heat had brought on a severe asthma attack, and Mother had been inhaling the sticky smelling smoke all morning.

Biff and I drank our coffee silently. Gee Gee poured herself a second cup and pulled her chair closer to ours.

"Why doesn't he ask us what he's going to ask us and get it to hell over with?" she said irritably. "This damn suspense is driving me nuts."

She spilled her coffee as she lifted the cup to her lips. It spattered on the table and Biff helped her wipe it up.

"If you hadn't lied in the first place . . ." He started to say more, but Gee Gee interrupted him.

"I didn't lie," she screamed. Her cup went crashing to the ground. The hot coffee splashed her bare legs and her kimono. She didn't seem to notice it. "How did I know Evangie was going to say it was her gun? Why should I go around talking about a gun anyway? That'd be bright dialogue, admitting I had a gun when there's a guy in our bathtub that's been shot with one."

She began wiping her leg with a paper napkin. She picked up the dusty cup and slammed it on the table.

"Seems there's a hell of a lot more lying being done around here than I'm guilty of. What the hell for? If nobody knows who the corpse is or who killed him, why do they lie? I seem to be the only one who had a reason for lying. Evangie says she didn't want Gyp's name to get in the newspapers. Well, I think that's a helluvan excuse for setting fire to the woods and burying a body. Then she says she thought it was Gyp's gun. Well, you can believe her if you want to. She's your mother, not mine. I'll be a son of a bitch if it sounds kosher to me."

She jumped up and ran into the trailer.

Mother hadn't moved during the tirade. When the door slammed she lifted her head.

"That's gratitude for you," she said. "After all we've done for that girl."

Mamie poured more powder on the burning mound. She picked up Gee Gee's cup and dropped it into the dishpan. Mandy grabbed the dish towel and dried the cups and saucers as Mamie washed them. The uncomfortable silence was shattered by Dimples's voice.

"Will somebody fix me a bromo?" she yelled from the trailer. "So help me, I think they tried to poison me last night."

Mamie filled a glass with water, picked up another clean one, and went into the trailer. It was going to take more than one Bromo Seltzer to cure Dimples, I thought. She had made enough the night before at a nickel a drink to retire with a hot-dog stand. If she had been trying to win the crown from Joyce, it looked as if she had it in the bag.

Her voice rose petulantly from the trailer.

"Dammit all, you don't have to look at me like that. So I got a hangover, so what? Just because you got a hollow leg is no sign I have."

I wondered if she meant Gee Gee or Mamie. Thinking about what she had said the night before, I settled for Mamie.

"I'll go dig up Corny," Biff said. He went to the bedroom. In a few moments he had Corny up and out. It was the sheriff's fault that Corny was still sponging on us. The comic wore Biff's bathrobe. Mandy's slippers were on his feet. He sank into a chair and sulked.

"So the long arm of the law wants our little party together eh?" he said sarcastically. "Well, he's got us. So what's he going to do for an encore?"

I poured him a cup of coffee and pushed the can of milk and the sugar bowl toward him.

"I'm sure I can't tell you that," I said pleasantly. "I know what he's doing for an opening, though."

Corny looked up from his cup of steaming coffee. I had tried to put a note of mystery in my voice. It must have been a good performance. He knew I had something on my mind, and I let him wonder for a second. I poured a cup of coffee for Biff and one for myself. I took my time adding the sugar and milk.

"I think he's going to ask you how your handkerchief happened to be buried with the body," I said.

"My what!" Corny jumped to his feet. "Where is he?" he screamed. "I gotta talk to him. I gotta tell him I don't know anything about it. Somebody's trying to frame me, that's what it is. Somebody's trying to pin this thing on me."

"You'll get your chance to talk to him," Biff said. "I wouldn't lean too heavy on that framing gag, though. I tried to give it to him last night, and he won't sit still. All of a sudden he don't like actors."

Corny sank back into his chair. He reached for the coffee cup. Then he pushed it away.

"Gimme a drink, will ya?" he asked.

If he had asked me I would have refused him. Biff is a softie, though. He got out the bottle and poured a double hooker in a water glass. Corny downed it in one gulp. Biff poured him another.

A voice from behind made me jump. It was one of the sheriff's men.

"The sheriff wants to talk to Miss Graham," he said. "In the office." He tossed a thumb toward the small building near the shower house. It was the same building from which I had telephoned the doctor.

"She's inside," I said. "I'll get her."

Gee Gee sat on the foot of the daybed. She had been crying. When I spoke to her I saw how bloodshot her eyes were.

"They want to talk to you first," I said. The desperation in her quick glance toward the door made me soften my voice. "Just tell them the truth, honey. Do you want a nip first?"

She shook her head. Without speaking she left the trailer. From the window I saw her leave with the man. They walked toward the office.

Dimples pulled herself from the bed. She reached for the leftovers of the Bromo Seltzer and drained the class.

"Of all the times for me to have a headache," she said. "I hope to Gawd they don't expect me to make sense when they start askin' me questions. Hell's bells, I don't know a thing about it. Never even knew there was a body until I heard Corny and your mother talking about it."

She hadn't washed off her body paint and in the morning light it looked pale green. Where she had perspired under her arms and between her full breasts the paint had runned off and her pink flesh showed through. She still wore her stage face makeup. The lip rouge had run down the corners of her mouth and her eye shadow was streaked across her forehead.

I handed her the can of cleansing cream and a box of Kleenex.

"They might ask for you next," I said. "If they ever see you looking like this they'll probably throw you in the clink on general principles."

She rubbed the cream on her face listlessly.

"What kind of questions do they ask?" she said a moment later.

"I dunno," I said. I was thinking about Gee Gee. I wondered if she would tell them about Mother thinking the gun was mine. I hoped not. It sounded flimsy. Even if it were true, it didn't sound right. Why would Mother try to conceal the gun because it had belonged to me? Unless she thought it was the murder weapon. But then, I reasoned, she would have to think I was the murderer.

"Will they ask me, 'Where were you on the night of—' Say when *was* he killed?" Dimples turned her greasy face toward me. She sat up straight and pulled herself up in the corner of the bed, her back leaning against the wall.

"I oughta know a few things about this," she said. "I'll look like a dope saying, 'I dunno, I dunno' all the time."

"I'm afraid we'll all look like dopes," I replied. "You know as much right now as I do. There was a corpse in our bathtub. Period."

Dimples was silent for a few minutes. I walked over and looked out the window. The door to the office was closed.

"They're talking an awfully long time," I said.

"It just don't make sense," Dimples exclaimed suddenly. "Who in the hell would put a dead body in our trailer? Of all the good places to hide it, they pick on a bathtub. Any damned fool would know we'd find it *sometime*."

"Maybe they wanted us to find it," I said. I spoke without thinking.

The office door had opened, and Gee Gee had walked out into the sunlight. She stood on the top step with her hands in her kimono sleeves. She looked around as though she couldn't decide which direction to take. Suddenly, with long strides, she began walking toward our trailer.

"*Wanted* us to find it?" Dimples said stupidly. "I don't get that, either. *Wanted* us to . . ."

"They probably just wanted to get rid of the body," I said. "They maybe thought we were traveling on, like we were, and that it was a good chance to put a lot of distance between them and their damn corpse. Instead of the murderer leaving town, he just sent the body out of town."

"I'll tell 'em when he comes in," Dimples said ironically. "I still don't get it. It's screwy. A guy kills a guy. He looks around for a place to dump the body. He sees us living in a trailer, minding our own business, and he says, 'That's for me.' He dumps the body in our bathtub and calls it a day. Why, all we gotta do is think back a little and think of who *could* dump a corpse in our trailer. When were we out of it long enough? Who had a key to unlock the door? Who'd be around a trailer camp in the first place? It's too easy."

"Too easy," I said slowly. "Well, let's start from A. We're in and out of the trailer all the time. How could we figure out which time the murderer decided to drop his load of sunshine? B is easier. We only leave the trailer for hours at a time. We only leave it alone until four, five in the morning when we go nipping. He'd only have hours to do it. C stands for cinch. What key for what lock? We haven't locked the trailer since we lost the keys in Los Angeles. As for asking who *could* dump the body in the tub, anyone in any town we've stopped in could have done it."

Dimples threw her legs over the side of the bed. She groped around on the floor for her pink mules. When she found them she pushed them on her feet with an indifferent movement. Then she threw her robe over her shoulders and picked up a Turkish towel.

"I'm gonna take a shower," she said. "You make my head ache with your alphabets. The way I feel now, I'll settle for Corny being the murderer. All I want is to get the damned thing cleared up. Who did it or why they did it is none of my business, and when the sheriff asks me where I was on the night of so-and-so, I'll tell him to go fuddle his duddle."

As she left the trailer, Mamie came in. She turned down the bedcovers and began tidying up the room. She was unconcerned, as though a corpse in the bathtub went with the plumbing fixtures. She put the cleansing cream and the Kleenex back in the drawer and dusted off the furniture carefully. She hung up the clothes that Dimples had left strewn about.

"I don't know how your poor mother can stand all this," she said as she rolled up a pair of nylons. "All the drinking and swearing and excitement. No wonder she has asthma."

"Well, things aren't always as upset as this," I said. "Sometimes we go for a whole week without finding one single corpse."

I might just as well have been talking to myself. Mamie was not interested in what we found in our bathtub. She was house cleaning, and that was all that mattered to her at the moment. Before she actually swept me out, I left.

Corny was leaving with the sheriff's man. They were half-way to the office, and I could still hear Corny's voice. It was shrill and piercing.

"It couldn't have been my handkerchief," he said almost hysterically.

Gee Gee and Mandy had started a pinochle game. She was dealing the cards as though nothing had happened. An empty whisky glass was at her elbow.

"How did it go?" I asked.

She put down the deck of cards and picked up her hand. Before she answered me she sorted her cards.

"Nothing to it," she said casually.

A nine of hearts was face up on the table. Mandy showed a nine from his hand and wrote down ten points under his name on the score card. He played a jack of clubs. Gee Gee took his trick with a king. She had no meld.

I suddenly dreaded more than ever my meeting with the sheriff. When Gee Gee plays a king on the first trick without a meld in her hand she isn't as composed as she is pretending to be. Gee Gee usually plays a good game of pinochle.

15 IT WAS ALMOST TWO HOURS BEFORE THE SHER-iff sent for me. Two hours of watching one after the other walk across the field to the office, two hours of waiting for the door to open and watching one more of our troupe walk slowly back to the trailer.

When Mandy was called I took his pinochle hand. Biff joined us later, and we played four handed. I'm sure the game was the only thing that kept me from going raving mad.

If anyone had been able to tell me what was going on, if all of their remarks weren't so much alike, I wouldn't have minded the wait as I did. They were all as evasive as Gee Gee had been.

They had all been asked if they recognized the corpse. They were expected to read a carefully written description, a full page in long hand, and to base their recognition on that. They had been asked how long they knew Biff and me, how long they had known Mother, how long they had known each other, how much they contributed toward the upkeep for the trailer.

That question in particular I thought was stupid. Aside from an occasional bottle, no one had contributed anything.

They were shown the gun and asked if they had seen it before, if they knew a man named Gus, if they had lost any articles of wearing apparel or laundry. They were asked if they had heard anyone or seen anyone prowling around the trailer.

It all sounded very silly to me. Even Biff could contribute a little more. I didn't like the way he smiled at me when it was my turn. I didn't like the way he said, "Just tell 'em the truth, honey."

I didn't like the silence of the sheriff's man as we walked toward the office, either. He was dripping wet with perspiration. It was close to noon, and the thermometer had been passing the one-hundred mark since morning. However, the heat was the least of my worries. With the heat you know that sooner or later it's going to cool off. It's like having a hangover; you know you won't suffer forever. The past two hours had seemed an eternity to me. I couldn't believe that the ordeal would ever end.

The shades were partly drawn in the small, hot room. The sheriff sat directly in front of an electric fan. A bent blade kept up a steady offkey clinking sound as it hit the wire guard.

The sheriff motioned for me to sit across the table from him.

"Would you like the fan turned in your direction?" he asked when I wiped my face with a limp handkerchief.

I shook my head.

"It only churns up the same old hot air," I said. "No offense meant with that hot-air crack." I added.

The sheriff fumbled with a piece of wrinkled paper.

"Look," I said, "if that's the description of Gus or that other dead man, I don't know anything about it. I told you all I know about Gus and I never knew the second one."

The sheriff let the paper fall from his hand. He reached for the cardboard box. It looked rather the worse for wear now.

"And," I said, "if that's the gun, don't wear yourself out with opening up the box. First time I saw the gun in my life was when Joyce Janice handed it to Mother at The Happy Hour saloon. I told you that before."

I leaned back in my chair, feeling quite pleased with myself. I was beginning to understand why Gee Gee and the others had said there was nothing to it.

The sheriff poured himself a cup of water. As an after-thought, he offered it to me. I refused. Effectively, too, I thought. With a half smile, I merely shook my head. The sheriff looked at me. I had a fleeting thought that I had done something that amused him. I had an idea that he was laughing to himself. I didn't like that, either.

"Here's something that might interest you," I said. "Last night when Biff and I left your charming office, we walked back toward the saloon section. When we passed the doctor's house we heard a car start up. It was a big, light-colored car and it left from the doctor's driveway. Cullucio was driving it. He was in a hurry, too, and he had been calling on the doctor."

"And how do you know that?" the sheriff said slowly. "He could have been calling next door, couldn't he?"

"Yes," I agreed ungraciously. I didn't like the interruption and, most of all, I didn't like the smile on the sheriff's face. "Only at the moment he left, the doctor's lights went out and Biff and I heard him lock his door. Cullucio isn't the type to pay a social call at almost one in the morning. He couldn't look healthier, so what's he doing visiting a doctor? A doctor who's a close friend, obviously of the local law? Of course, you prob-ably know all about it, but The Happy Hour is certainly not a very choice spot. The boss is hardly the sort to get chummy with the law, if you know what I mean."

I took a cigarette from the package in my pocket and lit it slowly. I was feeling more and more pleased with myself. I liked the look of astonishment on Hank's face, too. After one or two puffs on my cigarette, I let my eyes go big.

"I should have asked permission first," I said, glancing down at the cigarette. "Maybe smoking isn't allowed during the third degree."

"It's quite alright," the sheriff replied stiffly.

"Is there anything else you want to know?" I asked.

"Noooo. I thought you might like to have me explain one or two points, though," the sheriff said.

I most certainly did but I wouldn't give him the satisfaction of knowing that. I smoked quickly. The cigarette burned too fast and, as I inhaled, the hot smoke burned my throat. I wanted a cup of water desperately but, after my big head-shaking, slow-smiling scene a moment before, I didn't have the nerve to mention it.

"We're right on the border here in Ysleta," the sheriff said. "A few years back they used to allow gambling on the other side. That brought in a bad element and, even though we've worked hand in glove with the Mexican government, it seems we can't get rid of the element. Tourists flock here during the season to see these places. Nothing for 'em to see but a bunch of saloons like they can see any place else, but as long as they keep coming there'll always be guys around to clip 'em. During the last few months a new menace has cropped up. It's a dope racket. The difficult part of all of it is that the dope is grown right here in Texas. It's known as a weed, of course, it's cultivated here. Loco weed, the natives call it. The proper name is marijuana."

"Reefers!" I said. As I spoke I could almost see Gee Gee's face when she was telling me about Gus.

"Yes," the sheriff replied. "It's sent out of this state in bales, fifty- and hundred-pound bales. We got one of the trucks but we couldn't hold the driver. He said it was given to him. His instructions were to carry it as far as Galveston, then it was to be picked up. If it were just marijuana, it wouldn't be so bad. People say marijuana isn't habit forming. I have my own ideas on that score, but most folks say the danger in smoking these cigarettes is that, after a while, people become immune to its influence. They take up cocaine, and from there it's only a step to heroin. Sometimes these dealers spike the cigarettes with hashish or the scrapings of opium bowls. That's done to get customers in the habit."

"You oughta write a book about it," I said.

"I have," the sheriff replied.

I was sorry I mentioned it. The gleam in the sheriff's eye told me he was on his favorite subject. I still wanted a cup of water, and my cigarette had smoked down to a short butt that was burning my fingers. It seemed disrespectful to drop it on the floor, but I did. Then I ground out the glow with the toe of my shoe.

"The head of the narcotic division in Austin traced the source of supply to my section," the sheriff said. His bushy eyebrows drew together in a frown. "I followed a lead as far as The Happy Hour. Then I lost it. We found a small tin of heroin in one of the employees' possession. The man was completely under the influence of drugs, and we couldn't get a thing out of him. That's as far as I got with my lead. I've watched the mail; I've watched every employee. Nothing incriminating about any of 'em. Nothing but that tin of dope. Yet I know for a fact that someone at The Happy Hour is responsible for part of this dope peddling."

The sheriff sighed heavily. His fingers drummed on the table before him. Had I not remembered how rude he had been to Biff and me the night before, I would have felt sorry for him.

"Now these murders," the sheriff said. "They must be mixed up with the business in some way."

His hands were still now. Then he pounded on the table until I thought it was going to break into splinters.

"But I'll find the guilty one," he said.

"Well, don't look at me, brother," I said. "I just got into town."

"I know," the sheriff said. "So did the corpse. And not long after you all arrived we found another corpse. Then there's a little matter of untruth. That Graham girl, for instance. It was stupid of her not to come to me immediately after finding the body. She should have told me about the Gus business in Los Angeles . . ."

"Wait a minute," I said. "I've trouble enough sticking up for my mother without making alibis for friends, but how was Gee Gee supposed to know you were looking for reefer peddlers? She sees a dead guy in a bathtub. She knows him. She has reasons maybe for wanting him out of the way. Under those circumstances I don't blame her for keeping her mouth shut."

"Reasonable enough," the sheriff said, nodding his head slowly. "In any other case than a murder case. I understand you and your husband were mixed up with a murder case once before . . ."

"Not exactly mixed up. Biff only found the murderer, that's all."

If I expected a look of respect for Biff after my announcement, I certainly would have been disappointed. The sheriff brushed away my statement as though it were an everyday occurrence for a burlesque comic to find a murderer. His mind was on facts, he said rather coldly, not fancy.

"I'm not going to discuss your mother at all," he said, "other than to mention the fact that she lied about the gun. As for these three people traveling with you to open an engagement at The Happy Hour, well I guess work is work, but I didn't think any self-respecting, decent people would play a nightclub like The Happy Hour."

"There's nothing wrong with The Happy Hour that a police clean up wouldn't cure," I said. It wasn't the thing to say, but it was too true for me to let the chance slip by.

"What about Corny Cobb? Is he the type of person a couple of honeymooners would invite along for the trip?" the sheriff asked.

"You don't know my husband," I replied. There must have been a weary note in my voice.

The sheriff dismissed me. For the time being, he added hastily. He saw me to the door and spoke in an undertone to the two men who were waiting outside. I didn't hear his words, but I knew he was asking them to bring someone else in for questioning.

The picture that greeted me when I returned to the trailer was a familiar one. Gee Gee was still playing cards with Mandy and Biff. Corny was tenderly nursing a drink. Dimples was plucking her eyebrows. The mirror hung from the doorknob of the front door, and Dimples sat on the top step. Mamie stood by, stage managing the beauty operation.

"You're not doing it right," she said. "Why don't you girls let me do these things for you? I'll admit the only training I've had was a mail-order house, but I have had a lot of experience. For instance, you should put alcohol first . . ."

"I wouldn't waste it like that," Dimples muttered. "And what's more, I like to do it myself. A smart guy once told me it had something to do with masochism or something. Anything that goes by a handle like that is for me."

Biff got to his feet and yawned loudly. "Think I'll go for the papers," he said.

The mail delivery was at noon, and the trailer post boxes were at the bend of the road. Biff whistled softly as he sauntered down the road.

I thought it strange that no one had asked me anything about my interview with the sheriff. They seemed to take it as a matter of course that nothing new had happened. The thought disappeared and another took its place. The new thought was an uncomfortable one. It made me tingle as though my feet had gone to sleep.

The tingling traveled slowly up my spine. I suddenly wanted to yell to Biff. I wanted to tell him not to leave me, that I was going to need him. I knew something was going to happen and, whatever it was, I didn't want to be alone when it did.

If Mother hadn't called me from the trailer, I would have followed Biff down the road, but Mother's voice sounded so urgent. "Is that you, Louise?" she asked.

She opened the bedroom door and stood on the top step. Her face was swollen and tired looking. The bright sunlight made her eyes water; her breathing was heavy. Even as she mumbled down the steps and walked toward me she spoke hurriedly.

"What did the sheriff say to you?" she asked. "Did he say anything about me?"

I've never seen Mother look so ill. I put my arms around her trembling shoulders and tried to force her gently into the chair.

"He didn't ask me anything new," I said soothingly, "just the usual things. Certainly nothing to upset you like this."

Mother pushed me away. Her face was crimson. Small beads of sweat covered her forehead.

"You're lying!" she shrieked. "Everybody's been lying to me right along. Even my own daughter is against me!"

Great blue veins stood out on Mother's neck. Her eyes searched my face frantically. When I tried to hold her, she swung her arm about. Her fingers were like claws as they clutched at the air.

Mandy jumped to his feet, upsetting the cards and Corny's bottle. He ran over to Mother and tried to help me hold her, but Mother scratched at him and pounded his arm with her fist. Mandy drew away and looked around helplessly.

Gee Gee and Dimples were frozen to the spot. So was Mamie. They didn't try to hold Mother back as she ran toward the office.

"I've got to talk to him again," she screamed as she ran. "I've got to tell him everything before it's too late."

Gee Gee grabbed my arm and held it so tightly I could feel the blood leaving my hand. "Let her get it off her chest," she said. "Maybe she really does know something."

"Let go of me," I heard myself say. "She's sick. Can't you see that?"

I wrenched my arm away from Gee Gee and ran toward the office. When I was still a hundred yards from it, I saw the door close behind Mother. I ran faster until I could feel the knob under my fingers. I turned it and tried to open the door. It was locked.

"Let me in," I screamed. "She doesn't know what she's doing. Don't listen to her."

The door remained closed. I ran around to the side of the cabin and pounded both fists on the window. There was no answer. I beat on the windowsill until my hands felt raw. The rough wood of the sill left splinters on my knuckles and a broken fingernail hung loosely from the cuticle. It began to bleed as I stared down at it stupidly.

Then I heard the door open. I ran around the small building and into the room.

Mother stood at the door. The sheriff and two men stood near her.

"You're too late Louise." Mother was calm, too calm. It was as though she were in a trance. "I've told them everything. I couldn't keep quiet any longer. They would have found out anyway, and I think it's better this way."

Mother smiled up at the sheriff. It was a sad little smile that made my heart skip a beat.

"Shall we go now?" she asked in a small, childlike voice. Mother turned to me then. "No one will blame me for killing them when they know the truth," she said simply.

The sheriff took Mother's arm and helped her to the car. She waved to me as she sat next to him in the front seat. She went on waving to me until the car was out of sight.

16

BIFF RACED THE MOTOR FOR A MINUTE. THEN he let it idle as he held both my hands tightly.

"Pull yourself together, Punkin," he said. He had said it many times before. It wasn't the repetition that annoyed me; it was the coaxing note in his voice. I tried to pull my hands away, but he held them tighter.

"This throwing your weight around isn't helping Evangie any," he said. "Instead of following them this minute, you oughta lie down and rest a while. Have a cup of tea or a drink . . ."

"Oh, stop babying me!" I said. "It's all right for you and Gee Gee and Dimples and everybody to keep on saying 'pull yourself together.' It isn't your mother who's sitting in jail with a murder charge hanging over her head. It isn't your mother who confessed to something she didn't do just because it was forced out of her. I think you all *want* to believe she did it. It's easier than having the cops suspect you. And that goes for the whole damn bunch of you, too. I'm going to my mother and I'm going right now."

"Very well then," Biff said quietly. "I'll drive you."

"You can drive or get out. It doesn't make any difference to me."

"Look," Biff said after a moment. "No one forced Evangie into anything. She said what she wanted to say when she wanted to say it. And it seems to me she has enough on her mind without you doing a free Bernhardt for the cops. Save that talent for the theater; a little of it wouldn't hurt your career a bit. And where do you get that 'she's not your mother' dialogue? Just because they put an in-law handle after it is no sign she isn't my mother, too. I got her when I married you. From now on remember that she's as much my mother as she is yours."

Biff shoved the truck into gear and faced toward the main road. For a moment I thought he deliberately drove through every rut and bump. Then I looked at his face. I had never seen his jaw set so firmly. I felt suddenly ashamed of my outburst.

"It wasn't only you," I said, "but the others, too. You didn't see them or hear them like I did. They acted like they almost expected Mother to confess. Even Gee Gee was funny about it, and Corny, with his ugly, gloating face, smiling to beat hell. He was glad, I tell you, really glad. I could have killed him. I think I would have, too, if Mandy hadn't pushed him away from me. Then you, instead of helping me, what do you do? Nothing, that's what. You waste hours talking about it instead of getting to her."

"It was ten minutes, not hours," Biff said. "Confession or no confession, they won't hang her before we get there. Now shut up and light me a cigarette."

I felt in his breast pocket for the package. The cigarettes were damp and spongy. The matches were too wet too ignite.

"You'll have to smoke one of mine," I said. "These are soaking wet."

"Now you're going to beef about that, I guess," Biff said. "A guy can't even sweat anymore. His wife has hysterics all over

Restful Grove, and a guy's not supposed to sweat a little. Nice thing."

His eyes were still on the road ahead and his chin still jutted out belligerently, but there was a satisfied half smile in his voice. I lit two cigarettes and handed him one. Over the bearing knock of the motor I heard him mumble thanks and then the radiator boiled over. A thin geyser of rusty water splattered on the cracked windshield, and Biff set the wiper in motion. I listened to the steady click-clack as the rubber flange raced back and forth in front of my eyes.

"Feel all right now?" Biff asked.

I didn't answer him. It didn't seem necessary.

"Well, then, we better get a couple of things straightened out before we see the sheriff," Biff said. "First of all, no jokes with him. Let him say his piece and don't interrupt him. I don't know if you've noticed it or not, but don't add anything but yes or no to 'em. Let him do the figuring. There's a couple things I don't like about this business. It doesn't seem right to me that he should bundle Evangie up in the car and drive her away without checking her story with the rest of us. He's got something up his sleeve, and I'll be damned if I like it."

"I tried to tell you he forced the confession from her," I said.

"You were right outside the door," Biff said patiently. "Evangie was in there for five minutes? No, I got two ways of looking at that confession. One is that she did it because she thought you killed the guys . . ."

"*Me?*"

"You don't have to be dumbfounded about it. She's got plenty of reasons for thinking that. The handkerchief had your name on it. So I know all about the laundry being sent out with your name, but the sheriff doesn't know it. We told him, that's all. She might wonder why you didn't admit knowing Gus. You played the Burbank Theater. Gee Gee said he was around there all the time. Evangie knows what a sucker you are for a bargain, and there's that guy selling stuff for nothing and you aren't in on it. That alone looks bad. She knows how you are; hot or cold, if thing's cheap, you'll go. The gun thing; she thought it was yours, so she tried to ditch it."

"Well, the gun *wasn't* mine. And if Mother would think that just because I'd played the Burbank I'd know Gus, then she'd think that all of us knew him. You played the Burbank, you didn't know him. Corny played it, he didn't know him. Dimples played it, she didn't know him . . ."

"Yes, she did," Biff said. "But that's beside the point. I'll get around to Dimples later. Right now I'm talking about you. The cops don't know your sweet, sunny disposition. They want a murderer. Your mother gets frightened and gives 'em one. That's the way it goes if she didn't kill the guys herself, but you'll have to admit that her killing 'em is the easiest thing to believe. Aside from great great grandmother with the human steaks and poor Uncle Louie with the tattoos. Evangie's got the guts to kill a guy. She proved that when she buried the body. That wasn't kid stuff, ya know. Think about the strange way she's acted since San Diego. That could be explained if she knew the body was in the bathtub. You can't act natural with a thing like that on your mind.

"Why didn't she want us to call the cops? Why did she want to bury the body and drive away? She recognized the handkerchief with a quick glance. How? There's only one way she could tell that that handkerchief was Corny's. Gyp, I hate to say it, but I've got the damndest feeling that she knew about the second corpse. I don't say she killed him, mind you, but . . ."

"But you think she did."

Biff leaned forward and turned off the windshield wiper. Then sudden silence made me want to scream.

"You think she is a murderer," I said.

Biff's hand fell on my knee. I felt him shake me gently.

"No encores with the dramatic scene, Punkin," he said. "Smoke the cigarette and take it easy. I'll put it to you like this: What do you think Evangie would do if someone threatened her? Or you? What if someone tried to blackmail her, not about herself, but about you? Say a guy tells her that he knows something ugly. He says he'll blab to the papers if she doesn't pay up. Maybe he says he'll blab anyway. Spite or something. I know what she'd do. What do you think?"

"I-I think she'd kill him," I said. The smoke from my cigarette was curling up into my eyes. I opened the window a crack and let the cigarette fall.

Biff drove on silently, and I looked out the dusty window at the monotonous view ahead. I had thought the country was romantic when we first arrived in Texas. The yucca had been in blossom then and the splashes of red across the desert had looked like small bonfires. Now they were gone and there was nothing to relieve the parched, hot look of the sand. A breeze rolled a branch of sagebrush across the road. It seemed like a living thing, a living thing that couldn't make up its mind which way to roll. It suddenly was tossed under the wheels of the truck and I could almost feel the pain of its being crushed.

"No," I said. "Mother could shoot a man, I think, but she couldn't stab him in the back. If she shot him, it could be in self-defense, but if she stabbed him it would . . ."

"It could still be self-defense," Biff said. "At least to a jury."

A jury! I hadn't thought of that. Mother on trial for her life! The realization that this wasn't just another of Mother's difficult situations made my hands tremble. This wasn't something that Mother could smile her way out of. It wasn't a piece of stolen wardrobe or a steamed-open letter; it was murder. What if they found her guilty?

"She could have stabbed him in a moment of panic," Biff said. His voice sounded strange to me, as though I had never heard it before.

"Just because the knife was in his back is no sign that she sneaked up on him or anything. He could have been reaching for a weapon even, and when he turned she . . ."

Biff stopped talking suddenly. I knew that he didn't believe what he had been saying.

I watched the heat rise in small ripples on the road ahead of us. The radiator had begun to boil over again and almost unconsciously I leaned forward and started the wiper in motion. We passed a sign that read dip, and Biff put out his arm to hold me as we reached the depression in the road. I wanted him to hold me closer; the tenseness of his muscles seemed to give me courage, but he released me and clutched the wheel again.

"It wouldn't be hard for her to plead insanity, ya know," Biff said slowly. "It might be better than self-defense at that."

We had reached the outskirts of the town, and Biff slowed down. The traffic signs read: TWENTY MILES AN HOUR. DRIVE SLOW AND SEE OUR TOWN. DRIVE FAST AND SEE OUR JAIL.

Biff chuckled. "Fast or slow, it's all the same with us."

A second sign read: DRIVE SLOW, DEATH IS PERMANENT.

As we drove through town I noticed how small groups of men nudged each other as they followed our truck with their eyes. One man leaning against a signboard spat. The brown juice from his tobacco dripped down his chin and he rubbed it away carelessly. It was an ordinary gesture, but it was done too deliberately. The man's eyes were narrowed, and one hand fell significantly on the holster at his hip.

As Biff parked the car, the men who sat on the courthouse steps moved aside for us. They gave us too much room. Their eyes were hostile. They stopped talking when we approached them.

The two men who had been with the doctor when he examined the body were standing near the door. They looked at me for a moment, then let their eyes drop.

Biff opened the door for me, and as I walked through I could hear scraps of interrupted conversation.

"Never saw a burleycue show myself, but I sure heard plenty about 'em." The voice laughed obscenely.

"We had a troupe try to perform here once," another said. "We run 'em out fast." Under the slyness there was a hint of regret, I thought.

I turned around and faced the men.

"But you'll let creep joints stay open," I said loudly. "You don't pay any attention to dives like . . ."

Biff held my arm and pushed me ahead of him. He slammed the door behind us.

"Remember what I told you about losing your temper," he

whispered. "They want to get you riled up. Don't listen to 'em. And remember, let me do the talking."

The sheriff's voice boomed out.

"He's right about that all right." He laughed loudly and hit the palm of his hand on top of the desk.

The sheriff was alone. He sat behind his desk with his feet stretched out on the open drawer. An opened copy of *Variety* was tossed carelessly on the floor beside him. The scene was familiar, almost too familiar. Even the sun streaming in the window was part of a stage setting that I had worked in before.

The sheriff jumped to his feet and pulled over a chair for me. He pushed another toward Biff.

"Before we go into the complaints about the Chamber of Commerce," the sheriff said, "we'll have a little drink."

He put the same bottle of liquor on the desk and next to it he placed three paper cups.

"Say when," he said.

Biff frowned. Then he looked at me and shrugged his shoulders.

"When," he said. I noticed that he waited until the cup was full.

The sheriff handed me another cup and then he sat down and leaned back in his swivel chair. He downed his drink and let his eyes travel from Biff to me.

I put down my cup without touching it to my mouth. "Where's my mother?" I asked. "I demand a lawyer before she is questioned. If you have tried to make her admit something she didn't do, I'll—I'll—well, it's unconstitutional to question her without an attorney. She can swear that you tried to third-degree her or something. Even if she did do it, it's . . ."

Biff stood up and walked over to my chair. He grabbed my hand before I had a chance to pound it on the desk.

"Why don't you keep your big throat closed?" he said. He spaced each word with deep breaths. "The sheriff isn't giving free drinks to murderers' daughters. The gentleman must have something on his mind that's bothering him. Why don't you give him a chance to speak his piece?"

Biff sat on the arm of my chair and let his hand rest lightly on my shoulder. He spoke to the sheriff.

"Now that I have my wife muzzled, give us the story from the beginning. I know Evangie well enough to know that she didn't wait for any legal brain. She shot her bolt before she even got to this office. Right?"

The sheriff smiled. Then he nodded.

"Well," he said cautiously, "she did tell us a few things while we were driving in from Restful Grove, but the details we filled in after she got more comfortable here in the office."

He reached into the drawer and placed a sheaf of papers on the desk. He picked up the top one and read it to himself. Then he handed it to Biff.

"Recognize the handwriting?" he asked.

Biff glanced at the paper, then at the signature at the bottom. "Yes," he said.

"It's your mother-in-law's, isn't it?" the sheriff said.

Biff nodded and the sheriff went on.

"It's a signed confession to the murder of Gus Eglestrom, alias Happy Gus, alias George Murphy, alias—well, I won't bother you with all of 'em."

17 I WON'T GIVE YOU THE FULL TEXT OF THE CONfession, either," the sheriff went on. His eyes smiled as he looked over his desk at me.

"Your mother isn't exactly a woman of few words, you know. It took her ten pages to tell us what anyone else could have told us in two. Seems your mother met Gus Grange, that's another of the deceased's aliases, in 1913. He was a chiropodist. Your mother married him, but just before you were born this corn doctor takes it into his head that he doesn't like being a family man. He ups and leaves your mother. Then she meets the man you thought was your father. He asks her to marry him, but your mother can't because she has no trace of this Gus Grange. She foolishly tells this other man that her husband was dead. Why, I don't know.

"Anyway, a week before you're born, she gets news that Grange really is dead. He was reported to have been killed in a saloon brawl in Sitka, Alaska. Your mother married the other man, and, when you were born he gave you his name. Through all these years she kept this from you because she wanted you to remember the second man as your father. He loved you very much and it was his dying wish."

The sheriff stopped for a moment. He cleared his throat experimentally. Then he reached for the bottle and poured himself a drink. As an afterthought he poured one for Biff. Noticing that I hadn't touched mine, he told me to drink up.

I didn't want the liquor, but something in the sheriff's expression made me believe that it would be better to drink it. I couldn't taste it as it burned my throat.

"When did Mother find out that Gus—my father, I mean—was still alive?" I asked.

"Not until you started making money," the sheriff said. "Seems he recognized a picture in a newspaper, a picture of you and your mother. All of a sudden he decided that he still loves your mother very much. So much so, in fact, that he wanted her to come back to him, with you and your salary, of course. He can't understand why your mother doesn't want you to know that your real father is an ex-convict, that he's a cheap pickpocket, a fence, a dope peddler, and a panderer. He tells your mother that it's your duty to contribute to the support of your loving father.

"Your mother says that she'd see him in hell first, and he reminds her of how the story would look in print. So she pays him money each week. That goes on for a while, and then Gus decides he ought to have more money. His daughter is in the movies now. She's getting a bigger salary, and he naturally wants a bigger slice of it. He wants to live as he thinks the father of a movie actress should live. Your mother makes the mistake of ignoring his letters, so he follows you to San Diego."

Suddenly, as though he couldn't hold it in another minute, Biff said, "Then she did kill him in self-defense."

The sheriff ignored him. He picked up the second sheaf of

papers and flicked through the closely typewritten words. When he spoke his voice was husky.

"This is a signed confession to the murder of Captain Robinson, able-bodied seaman. The name captain is a complimentary title."

"That's the name of the captain who married Biff and me at . . ."

Biff grabbed my arm before I could finish. He walked over to the desk and looked at the paper the sheriff held.

The sheriff turned the pages back until he came to the last page. Then he showed Biff the signature. He held the paper up to me.

"Is that your mother's signature?" he asked.

It was written with a shaky hand. There was a blot of ink at the corner of the paper, but it was my mother's signature. I nodded.

Biff came over to my chair again and put his arm around my shoulder. His hand felt heavy, as though it were a detached thing.

"If he wasn't a captain, that means that Punkin and I aren't married."

The sheriff went on, "Well, yes, I guess that would be right. But let me finish. The captain was a friend of your father's. They'd been in a couple of scraps together and were in jail together for a while. The captain knows about Gus, your father, that is, blackmailing your mother. It was the captain who showed him the clipping about you getting married. Gus doesn't like the idea of your getting married a little bit. He figured that once you had a husband he'd take care of the business details, like collecting the salary and banking it and so on. It was easier, Gus thought, to keep on getting money from your mother than having to do business with a man.

"When he reads that you and Biff intend marrying at sea, it's a cinch for him to step in with his friend, the captain. He just followed you two around that night in San Pedro and when you happened to meet a man who knew 'just the captain,' it was him. He even called the Port of Authority too, as if a marriage beyond the three-mile limit was legal. At least, that's what he told you two."

"He called the number," Biff said quietly. "I spoke to the man in charge myself."

"You spoke to *a* man, your mother says. You didn't speak to *the* man."

"And Mother knew all the time that our marriage was illegal?" I asked.

The sheriff nodded.

"She tried to have you leave Biff, didn't she? She never left you alone with him for a minute, did she? Yes, according to her confession, she knew everything. Gus was the kind of man who bragged about his methods. It was during one of his more— aggressive moments that your mother . . ."

"That she shot him," Biff said tonelessly.

"After Gus was dead," the sheriff went on, "your mother thought that the blackmailing was over. She didn't reckon with Captain Williams. He took it up where Gus left off."

The sheriff's voice had become softer and softer. Finally I couldn't hear it at all. I felt myself slipping from the hot leather chair, lights were before my eyes. Then Biff's arms were holding me. The sheriff held a cup of liquor to my mouth. I must have swallowed some because I could feel the burning in my throat.

". . . shouldn't have told it like that," I heard the sheriff say. "When you said you wanted the story from the beginning, I gave it to you like you wanted."

The sheriff walked back and forth in the small room and spoke slowly. His boot spurs made a clanking sound as he walked. The bluebirds embroidered on the boot toes were covered with dust.

"That's just the way your mother told the story. I had two people taking it down word for word. She read the confession through and then she signed it. She seemed calm enough and she asked for a cup of water. I gave it to her myself. Then a funny thing happened.

"She took the cup from me and stirred up the water with her

finger. She kept turning the cup one way and then the other. Suddenly she turned it upside down on my desk and twisted it around again. The water spilled all over her and she didn't seem to feel it. There was something strange about the way she was holding her head, too, like she was listening for something. She looked up at me. Her eyes were almost closed. 'I think I see a gun in my cup,' she said. She handed me the empty paper cup and said, 'I can't read it well. You read it.'"

The sheriff turned his face from Biff to me.

"She must have thought it was tea," I said.

The sheriff nodded. He scratched the back of his neck with his huge hand. Then, with the same baffled expression, he said: "I've seen cases like this before, but I have to admit I didn't recognize the symptoms in your mother. They all have hallucinations, but they don't make their stories as plausible. They contradict themselves and get mixed up with the details. Usually their eyes are bloodshot, their hands are shaky. Their eyes are yellow rimmed, too. I should have known it. I should have known your mother was no coward. Only cowards allow themselves to be blackmailed. She would have told you about it from the beginning and asked you what to do. I don't think she'd stab a man in the back, either. Like I say, though, if I'd seen the pupils of her eyes, I might have guessed. She must have just taken it up."

"Taken what up?" I asked.

"Why heroin, of course," the sheriff replied. "Only I don't think it was all heroin. There was too much fantasy in the story for that. At a guess, I'd say hashish. They can really weave 'em on hashish. Why, I had a guy here once that convinced me he was . . ."

"What are you talking about?" I said. "My mother never took dope in her life. She's even afraid of asprin. Weave what story?"

The sheriff snapped his fingers with irritation.

"I'm getting so I can't tell a story straight to save my life. I should have started right out with telling you where your mother is. She's at the doctor's. He's got her under observation.

He just called me a while ago and said she was better, but she was plumb out of her mind this morning. All that rigamarole she signed was made up, made out of whole cloth.

"Far as I figure out, your mother never even knew those two men she said she murdered. It was easy for me to check on a few things, like when she married your father. They were married three years before you were born. She was never married before or after. Captain Robinson is a real captain, too. There's nothing illegal about your marriage. I even checked with your bank. They have no record of money being paid out regularly. If she had been paying blackmail she would have to have done it with cash, and each salary check has been sent intact. The checks have been made out for hotel bills, costumers, and things like that. They never once got a check made out to cash. But even before I checked her story, I knew something was wrong. That teacup thing was the tip-off. So I sent for the doc and he gave her an injection. It was something they use as a depressive, and in a minute she looks around the office here and says, 'Where am I?'"

"Then she didn't kill them?" Biff said.

"No more than your wife here did," the sheriff replied. "Where she got that story I'll never know. Neither will she. Always react like that. They never know when they snap out of it."

The sheriff placed the papers back in the drawer and slammed it shut. Then he turned a key in the lock. He closed the roll-top desk and locked that.

"Come-on," he said, helping me to my feet. "I guess you'd like to see her."

18 THE BOYS WHO WERE HOLDING DOWN THE courthouse steps eyed Biff and me furtively as we waited for the sheriff to lock the door to his office. I think they expected to see us wearing handcuffs, with a ball and chain on our ankles for good measure.

To put them at ease I pulled out my compact and took a quick look in the mirror. A quick one was all I could stand. My nose was shiny and the Texas dust had settled in little lumps on my sunburned face. My lips were dry with only an outline of rouge. I don't pride myself on being a beauty girl, but you can carry anything too far. I ran a comb through my bangs and pretended that I was interested in something that was happening down the street as I rubbed the melted lipstick across my mouth.

Biff spoke to the sheriff in a loud, too-hearty voice. "What'll it be, Hank, old boy? Do we walk or ride?"

"Now that's up to the little lady," the sheriff said, nodding in my direction.

"It was the "little-lady" dialogue that brought the men to their feet. If they had had any doubts about our standing with the sheriff, his genial smile dispelled them. With the precision of the Rockettes they rose and turned on the personality. They were prettier when they frowned, but I had an idea that if Biff and I wanted to stay healthy we should give them our entrance smiles. That is a fast, brilliant smile. The exit is a long, slow one.

Two of the men detached themselves from the group and ran toward the sheriff's parked car at the curb. They almost collided as they opened the doors for us. Then they stood back to make way for our parade. I could feel the eyes of the others following us as we walked down the steps toward the car.

Of all the days for me to wear my seat-warped tweed of slacks, I thought bitterly. A perfectly good pongee pair in the trailer at Restful Grove, and me doing an exit in these.

One of the men closed the car door behind me. He gave me a chewing-tobacco smile as we drove off.

"Cute kids," Biff said.

The sheriff chuckled. "It don't take 'em long to catch on. You'll have to admit that. It'll be all over town in an hour."

"In less than an hour," I said to myself.

The nudging of ribs as we passed the corner drugstore could be heard over the knock of the motor. The open mouths turned into broad grins. I wondered if Hank knew the power he had.

Biff was overplaying the big-friendship scene. He let one

arm rest on the sheriff's shoulder. The other hung limply over the open window; one of the sheriff's cigars was clutched between his fingers. If he had been a politician in a parade he couldn't have laughed more often or more loudly.

"If you heard this one, don't stop me," he said. "I like to listen to it myself."

I was glad I sat alone in the back seat. Biff's jokes can be pretty tiresome at times, and this was one of the times. The sheriff either thought Biff was the funniest man in show business or he was just being polite. He didn't laugh, he roared. That was all Biff needed. He went right through his act, even to the blackout.

It wasn't that good, I know, but they both laughed until we pulled up in front of the frame house with Dr. Gonzales's shingle waving in the hot breeze. Then, as he helped me out of the car, the sheriff sobered.

"Now be careful that you don't upset your mother," he said.

Biff had said the same thing earlier. It was plain that they still didn't realize what Mother could go through without becoming upset.

"She's a mighty fine little woman," the sheriff said.

He was beginning to convince anyone. I was beginning to see something else, too. If mother had any use for the Ysleta police department, she could have it for the asking.

The sheriff removed his hat as we walked into the doctor's house. He held it tightly with both hands. He tiptoed to a door and tapped lightly.

"Come in," Mother sang out.

The sheriff crooked a finger in my direction and stood aside so I could enter.

I don't know what I expected to see when I walked into the doctor's office. I'm sure I didn't expect the scene that greeted me. The books on shelves from the floor to the high ceiling, the dark, real leather chairs, the graceful draperies, the subdued light filtering through the Venetian blinds, and Mother, my poor little mother who mustn't be upset, sitting with an afghan robe around her feet, at a card table.

The doctor and several men I had never seen before sat opposite her. The doctor shuffled the cards. His dark hands moved quickly and expertly as the cards fell into place. He wore a black alpaca coat with a white shirt showing at the neck. The whiteness accentuated his swarthiness. When he smiled at Mother his teeth gleamed; he didn't smile at Biff or me, he greeted us professionally.

"Bedside manner," Biff whispered to me, "Ysleta style."

Mother smiled wanly at me from over a pile of poker chips. "Louise dear," she said. She held out her arms, and I walked over to her.

"Are you feeling alright mother?'

'Oh yes. These men have been so kind."

That was an understatement if I ever heard one. They weren't only kind, they were groveling.

"They've been teaching me how to play poker," Mother said innocently. "My, it *is* a complicated game. I told them I would rather play pachisi, but they told me if I was going to stay in Texas for any time at all I had to learn poker." Mother laughed gaily and went on, "I'm such a dummy, though. I guess I never will learn."

Her slender hand touched the pile of chips lovingly.

Biff and I gulped. Mother was the champion poker player of the troupe.

"And Biff," Mother said maternally, "my son." She held out a hand for him, too.

The sheriff pushed Biff toward her.

"Go to her," he whispered.

The note of reverence was almost too thick now. I couldn't blame Biff for thinking twice before he threw his arms around Mother's shoulders. The "my son" sounded mighty funny from where I stood. But not to the men who were listening. They glanced at each other with an "I'd-die-for-her" expression on their faces. They dropped their eyes and clenched their teeth when Mother said: "Thank heavens, my children are with me again." A big round tear fell down Mother's cheek, and she looked up at the sheriff without brushing it away.

"Is it—all over now?" she asked falteringly.

"You bet it is," the sheriff said.

"And can I go home?" Mother's face was radiant. She let her eyes rest on one man after the other until they had all seen the love light in them. Then she held out her hand to the sheriff.

"My friend," she said.

I had been looking at the same act all my life, but it was still good. Mother was a born actress, I thought. Then I wondered, wondered if it was *all* an act. If so, Mother had improved.

"I took the liberty of having one of my boys bring your own car around," the sheriff said. "The truck, I mean. I thought you folks might want to be alone for a little while."

Biff said, "That's mighty fine of you, Hank." Then he helped Mother to her feet.

The men jumped up and began digging in their pockets. They counted out bills and change while one of them counted Mother's chips. When they handed the money to Mother, she looked at them with wide eyes.

"What's this for?" she asked.

"Why, that's your winnings," one of the men said.

"You mean, we were playing for *keeps*?"

The men laughed sheepishly. I swallowed my gum.

"Who were those men?" I asked when we were seated in the truck. Mother was too busy counting her winnings to answer me immediately. She looked up for a second. Her forehead was creased from thinking so deeply, and she began counting on her fingers again.

"I think one of those men cheated me," she said.

"Who were they?" I asked, trying to keep my temper under control.

"Oh, they were just newspapermen," Mother said. "They wanted an inside story about the murders."

"You, uh, gave it to them?" Biff asked. He stared straight ahead as he spoke.

"Why, of course I did. I told them you were a big lumberman from Oregon. I didn't think it would sound good if they found out you were a burlesque comic. I told them everything. They wanted pictures, and the only one I had was that baby picture of you, Louise, so I gave it to one of the men. Let's see now, twenty-seven, twenty-eight, twenty-nine . . . Yes, I really do think they cheated me."

"A lumberman," Biff said incredulously. "From Oregon, yet."

"Is that the picture of me lying on my stomach on the white rug?" I asked.

"Now you made me lose count," Mother said pettishly. "I have to start all over again."

Mother counted and counted. The motor knocked. The radiator boiled. The windshield clacked.

"Lumberman," Biff repeated over and over. "Lumberman." He was still mumbling when we drove into camp.

Gee Gee had let out a yelp as the truck stopped, actors and animals piled out of the trailer like an old two-reel comedy.

"My goodness," Mother exclaimed. "You'd think I'd been to Europe or Siam or something."

"Evangie's back!" Dimples shouted.

Trailerites began gathering around the lean-to tent to add their congratulations. The attention put Mother in a special sort of heaven. She hugged and kissed Mamie and even blew a kiss to Corny. The dogs were whining and jumping up and down. Rufus Veronica, the monkey, squealed to be petted, and the guinea pig looked on with his little beadlike eyes glittering.

Mamie had just set her hair. It was plastered down flat against her small head, and she wore a pale-lavender rayon mesh cap to hold it. Between that and her old gingham dress flapping around her thin hips, she looked more and more like a real native of Oologah, or whatever the name of that place was. I was afraid she was going to cry, and I was right.

"Oh, I thought they'd never let you out," she sobbed, clinging to Mother's neck. She stood back and looked at Mother. Then she threw herself in a camp chair and cried even louder. "It would have been all my fault, too," she said between bellows. "I always bring nothing but bad luck to people and here I am doing it again . . ."

It was spoiling Mother's homecoming. Not because Mother

doesn't like to see people enjoy a good cry, as she puts it, but because Mamie and her hysterics were taking the center of the stage. I knew that by the time I had counted a slow ten, Mother would have a fainting spell or she would feel an asthma attack coming on.

It was an asthma attack, and she had it before I counted past six.

"Will you get my Life Everlasting please?" she asked Biff.

Mamie jumped up and wiped away a tear. "Let me get it. You just sit there and rest now."

In a minute she was back with the powder and had sprinkled some in a saucer. She touched a match to the mound and helped Mother cover her head with the Turkish towel. While Mother inhaled and wheezed, Mamie clucked in sympathy.

Mandy emerged from the trailer wearing his bathrobe and carrying a half-empty bottle of rye. His eyes looked sleepy and his hair was mussed. One side of his face was creased from lying on it.

"Why doesn't someone let me in on the news?" he said. He patted Mother's head gently. "Welcome home, baby," he said softly. Then to Biff, "How's it?"

Biff eyed the bottle. "Tough, Mandy boy, very tough. What I need is a little drink."

"Me, too," Mandy said as though it were a brand-new idea.

Corny got the glasses.

". . . now all we've got to do is find out where she gets the dope," Biff finished his story and the bottle at the same time.

For privacy we had gathered at the office. The sheriff had told Biff to keep the inside story of the confession from Mother, and that meant keeping it from Mamie, too. Biff didn't think that Mamie would deliberately tell Mother anything that wasn't good for her to know, but she was too emotional to trust, especially where Mother was concerned.

Dimples drained the last drop from her glass and eyed the empty bottle morosely. "Well, I guess it's up to me to fill it," she said tonelessly. "I'll go if somebody'll drive me."

"No," Corny said. "I'll go. You stay here."

He took the five-dollar bill from Dimples and left.

"He must be damned thirsty," Dimples remarked as the door slammed.

"Or curious," Biff added under his breath.

Gee Gee looked sharply at Biff as he spoke. Then she shrugged her shoulders. "It's none of my business, I guess," she said, "but I'll be damned if I trust that guy. From what you say about Evangie being on that stuff since San Diego . . ."

"I didn't say San Diego exactly," Biff said quickly. "I only said that she started acting funny about that time."

"Well, it's the same thing, ain't it?" Gee Gee said petulantly. "Always shooting off your big mouth. You never give anybody else a chance to talk. What I wanted to say was this: if Evangie started acting funny since San Diego, then she couldn't be getting the stuff from here. She either has it with her or—well, some one of us is giving it to her."

Biff searched her face for a moment.

Gee Gee's eyes met him and she said, "Look, just because I mentioned it don't go getting ideas that it's me."

"I wasn't," Biff said quietly. "I was thinking about something else."

He jumped up and started for the door. "Come on, Gyp," he said from over his shoulder, "I want to examine that pantry again."

I thought he had gone a little insane but I followed him. I was getting used to insanity by then. But I did venture a question.

"And what pantry are you referring to?"

"That pantry that had its door open the night you thought someone was in the trailer," Biff said in the same well-spaced, precise tone.

"Oh *that* pantry! The only pantry we ever had . . ."

Then I realized that he was being serious.

"Do you think the dope is in there? Do you think it was the murderer who was in the trailer with me? Oh, Biff, wait a minute. Don't leave me alone. Oh. I'm . . ."

Biff grabbed my arm and dragged me along. He was taking such big steps. I couldn't keep up with him. Suddenly he slowed down. As we approached the trailer he whistled a little tune. I recognized it as Mother's four-leaf-clover song:

"I know a place where the sun never shines . . ."

"No sense in getting them excited," he said between notes. "After all, the stuff can't walk away."

He was right about that, of course, but he forgot that it could be *carried* away.

19 MOTHER AND MAMIE HAD LEFT THE TRAILER. The burned-out powder was in the saucer and the towel was folded neatly beside it. A note written on brown wrapping paper was propped against the lamp: Have gone calling. Love, Mother.

"Probably telling the folks about me being a lumberman," Biff said. He rolled up the paper and carelessly shoved it into his pocket.

The screen door was closed but unfastened. Biff let the dogs out. Then he hooked the monkey to a chain on the hitch and entered the trailer. I followed him. The sun was sinking and it left shadows on the enamel top of the stove. There was a whiskey glass upturned near the coffeepot. A drop of liquor spilled over the shiny surface.

Biff wiped it up with his finger and smelled it.

"Looks like Mamie had herself a nip before they went calling," he said.

He opened the pantry door and looked inside. Everything was arranged neatly. The salt and pepper and things we used frequently were toward the right. In the back were the bulky supplies like flour and coffee.

Biff began piling the groceries on the stove. When the pantry was empty he lifted up the shelf paper and looked under that. Then he examined each package and jar before he put it back where it belonged. He emptied the coffee tin into a piece of paper. He went through everything just as carefully. A half loaf of bread caught his attention. He took a knife and removed the soft inside part, then he broke it up into small crumbs.

"They must have been frightened into hiding the stuff some other place," I said as Biff closed the pantry door.

"It certainly wasn't in any of those boxes or anything. Or it was such a little bit that it couldn't count."

"It only takes a little bit," Biff replied. He gave the guinea pig the bread crumbs, the crust he wrapped in paper and threw into the wastebasket.

"In case anybody asks us who ate the bread, all we say is 'mice.'"

"You say it to everybody but me!" Gee Gee stood on the steps, looking in at us. Behind her stood Mandy and Dimples. Mandy's mouth was wide open.

"Am I screwy or am I?" he asked. "Corpses I can understand, but what the hell you expect to find in the groceries is beyond me."

Biff sat down on the foot of the bed and rested his elbows on his knees. He paid no attention to the trio as they came into the trailer.

"It's got to be around here someplace," he said almost to himself. "Stands to reason they got it stashed where they can get it quickly. It costs too much dough to take a chance on hiding it out-of-doors."

"Well, what are we waiting for?" Gee Gee asked suddenly. "Let's tear the joint apart until we find it—"

She pulled off her beret and rolled up her sleeves. "I'll tackle the front room with Gyp. You three handle the bedroom."

Opening the closet door, she began dragging out the clothes. She threw them on the daybed carelessly.

"You examine 'em," she said to me, "and I'll get 'em out. Squeeze all around the hems and seams carefully. Pockets too. I read in the paper once where they smuggled dope across the border in heels of shoes even. Some dame had diamonds in the cavities of her teeth. They can't fool me, though. If it's here, I'm the little girl who'll find it."

We found everything but heroin or cocaine. We found sand from Santa Monica, stubs from the drive-in theater, crumbs from the nutburger, one false fingernail, sixteen cents in pennies, a dried-up martini olive, and $4,397 rolled up in a page of the *Racing Form* and tucked into a knothole in the back of the bedroom closet.

Mandy found the money. It was in small dirty balls. His hand shook as he counted it the second time. "Jeesuss, I never saw so much dough in one lump in me life," he said.

Dimples threw open the closet door and crowded her bulk inside the stuffy two-by-four room. She ran her hands down the sides of the walls and tapped with her knuckles on the ceiling.

"Maybe there's more," she said breathlessly.

Biff shook his head. "I don't think so," he said slowly, "and I don't think we'll find the stuff now, either."

He began tidying up the trailer, replacing the bureau drawers and hanging up the clothes. Mandy tried to help but he was too dazed. One hand was useless anyway, the money was gripped too tightly in it.

"Jeesuss, I could buy me a chicken farm or a selling plater," he mumbled.

"Yeah, you could," Biff said, "only you ain't. The dough goes to the cops and it goes to 'em tonight. We've had trouble enough without sticking out our chins for a lousy four thousand bucks."

"Four thousand, three hundred and ninety-seven, and if it's lousy, I'll still sit still for it," Gee Gee said grimly.

"It wouldn't be yours by any chance?" Dimples asked suddenly. Her eyes were unfriendly, and a hard line made her mouth. "You sure remember the amount close enough."

"If you didn't remember it so close yourself," Gee Gee snapped, "how do you know *I* did? If it was mine, I'd admit it, angel pants. For that kind of dough I'd take my chances."

"Chances on what?" Biff asked.

"Don't give me that," Gee Gee replied quickly. "You know damn well that dough came from the sale of the dope. Think you're playing with kids?"

Mandy handed the money to Biff reluctantly, as though he wanted just one more feel to convince himself that it was real.

Biff folded it carefully and shoved it in his back pocket. He put the spread back on the bed and punched up the cretonne pillows. Then he looked around the trailer to see if everything looked as usual.

"Not a word about this to Evangie," he said, patting his back pocket. "We'll go into the village for dinner, and I'll scoot over and see the sheriff while you're all eating. If it belong to any of you," he said, letting his eyes travel slowly from Gee Gee to Dimples and finally to Mandy, "you'd better tell me now."

"What about Gyp?" Mandy said, not maliciously, but as though it was as improbable for me to have that much money as it was for any of them.

"She's never had more than a quarter at one time in her life," Biff said. "Evangie sees to that."

Gee Gee lifted that glass from the lamp and touched a match to the wick. A yellow light flickered and brightened as she replaced the bulb.

"What's with the electricity?" Dimples asked. She turned up the light switch. There was a dull click but no light.

"It's the cord again," Gee Gee replied. "This time it looks like Rufus has been chewing on it or something. I saw it this afternoon and then when Evangie got home I was too excited to remember it."

I hadn't realized how late it was until darkness fell. Mother had never visited that long before. I was suddenly frightened. I felt as though I had been running. My breath was short.

"Why doesn't Mother come home?"

"She's probably around camp someplace," Biff said casually. "I'll go give a look."

"I'll go with you," Mandy said quickly. "With that dough, you ain't walking in the moonlight alone, brother. Not that I don't trust you or anything, but you never can tell what'll happen."

"How right you are," Biff said as they left. Gee Gee jumped up and locked the door behind them. She stood with her back braced against the wood-veneer paneling and looked down at her hands. They were trembling.

"I need a drink," she said.

"And me," Dimples said. "Say, what happened to that guy with my five bucks? He's been gone a couple hours. I tell ya I wouldn't trust him as far as I could throw this trailer. He's probably bending an elbow in some bar and guzzling up my five spot. I knew I should have . . ."

She stopped and stared at Gee Gee and me. We must have all felt it at the same time. It was a tight feeling of terror that caught my throat. I could feel a chill travel up my back.

"My Gawd," Dimples whispered, "he's killed her, too." She looked wildly around the trailer, then she ran her hands through her yellow, wiry hair and shrieked, "He's killed Evangie like he killed the others."

I pushed Gee Gee away from the door and threw it open. As I ran toward the office I heard her slap Dimples.

"Shut up," she said. "You're nuts. Stop it now."

The trailer park was dark. The dim lights from the trailers didn't travel any farther than their own doorsteps. Low murmurs from the various radios seemed to follow me as I ran toward the trailer I thought Mother might have visited. Little Johnny's father opened the door when I banged on it. He squinted out into the darkness.

"It's me," I said breathlessly. "Is my—have you seen my mother?"

"Well, no, I haven't," he said slowly. "I did see her this afternoon though. She was talking to some man in an automobile. Think she drove away with him, but I'm not sure. Why?"

"Was she alone?" I asked ignoring his question.

"Yes, I think she was. There's no trouble, is there? That sure was a terrible thing to happen to a sweet little woman like her. Imagine finding a body in your own bathtub! My wife and me was just listening to a report about it on the radio. My wife here has an idea about . . ."

I left the man talking to himself and ran on toward the office. I should have telephoned immediately, I thought, instead of wasting time with stupid questions. I had a numb feeling, but I kept telling myself that nothing had happened—nothing serious, that is. I had seen Mother get herself out of so many scrapes that it was silly for me to think that anything could happen now. But the numbness made me dizzy. A feeble light in the office window showed me I was heading in the right direction; it helped clear my head, too.

"Hello," I said to the operator. Then I gave her the number.

Then there was a click. Then I heard ringing. The doctor answered the phone. I had reached him so quickly that I didn't know what to say. At least I don't remember what I said to him. He told me later that I sounded very calm.

"She's all right," he told me. I do remember that. "She said she left a note for you. Didn't you get a note?"

"Yes," I said. "We found it. I'm sorry if I bothered you. We, I got a little nervous. So much happening and everything. Tell her to stay at the sheriff's and we'll pick her up."

I placed the receiver back on the hook and leaned against the mouthpiece. It was as though my legs had suddenly collapsed under me and I was hanging mid-air. I felt in my pockets for my cigarettes. Then I remembered that I left them on the stove. I remembered how frightened Dimples had been, too. I turned quickly to go back.

I'm sure I wasn't nervous when I went out into the darkness again. I closed the door behind me and walked briskly in the direction of our trailer. As my eyes became accustomed to the change, I thought I could see the outline of our house. It was so much larger than most house trailers and I thought I recognized the lean-to tent. It just seemed to be farther from the office than I thought it was. I couldn't remember walking that far.

It seemed to be getting darker, too. I stopped for a moment to get my bearings. Behind me the office light cast a weak glow. Ahead, there was nothing but darkness. I had a sudden impulse to run back to the office. There was light there, there was a telephone. Ahead there was nothing.

"Biff! Biff!" My voice startled me. It made me feel more alone to hear no answer. Then I ran. I ran as fast as I could right into the black void ahead. As I ran I heard myself screaming, "Biff! Biff!"

Why don't people in their trailers hear me, I thought. Where were the lights from them? Where was the sound of their radios?

I stopped still and held my breath. Then I began counting. "When I get to ten," I said, "I'll go back to the office and telephone. I'm just lost, that's all. One, two, three . . ."

I couldn't go on. I forgot what came after three. I forgot which way to turn to the office. Instead of running, I made myself walk very slowly, very quietly. I could feel the dust brushing against my ankles as I moved one foot after the other. My hands were before me as though I were playing blindman's buff.

Then my foot stumbled on the bundle. I knew it was a dead thing even before I leaned down and touched the sticky substance that was blood. My fingers were stuck together when I pulled my hand away. I knew they were red with blood but couldn't see them. All I could see were strange lights crossing each other in front of my eyes. White lights like small spots that were coming closer and closer.

Then I heard a mumble of voices, like the voices of the balcony boys urging me on during my specialty.

"There should be music playing," I said suddenly. "And I don't work in a white spotlight. I should have a surprise pink or a special lavender. There's no applause."

"Stop that gibberish, dammit." It was Biff's voice! I could feel him shaking me. "I won't have you fainting again. Come on, pull yourself together."

"There was only one spotlight now, and it was on the dead bundle at my feet. I felt Biff's hand turning my face away from the light that was centered on the ground.

"Don't go looking at it," Biff said gently. "We don't want any more trouble from you now."

I didn't have to look at it. I knew who it was, one glance had been enough. I think I knew even before I saw it in the light. In that one glance I had seen the knife gleaming as it stuck out of the man's back. The knife wasn't buried deeply. Hardly deep enough, I thought, to make him lie so still and quiet. His face was twisted and his eyes were open. They looked surprised.

"It must have hurt him, Biff." It was a silly thing for me to say but I knew Biff wasn't listening to me. He was listening to Mandy. I couldn't see him but I recognized his voice.

"He's cold and stiff," Mandy said quietly. "Look, he's still got the five spot in his hand. Look how he's holding it. Dimples can kiss that five goodbye. They'll never get it away from him now."

"Go on over to the office and call the sheriff," Biff said. "Gyp and I'll wait here."

Mandy went on talking as though Biff hadn't spoken. He tugged on the five-dollar bill. Then he tried to force the dead hand open. "Boy, now I know what they mean by death grip."

Biff had turned on his flashlight and I could see the look of wonderment on Mandy's face change slowly to fright, then terror.

"You mean I got to walk back there alone?" he asked.

"Either that or Gyp and I'll go and you can stay here with . . . him."

Mandy hesitated a moment. Then he got to his feet. "O.K., I'll go."

He whistled loudly as he walked away.

20 KEEP TALKING IF YOU'RE NERVOUS," BIFF said as Mandy started back to the office.

"I'll be running too fast for that," Mandy replied. Then he was gone.

Biff handed me the flashlight to hold as he bent over the body at my feet. He was careful not to touch it. He just looked at it silently. Then he handed me a handkerchief.

"Wipe off your hand, Punkin," he said.

All the red wouldn't come off. It was like makeup, I thought. Some blood was on the flashlight. I wiped that, too.

"Seems that he would have fallen on his face, doesn't it?" Biff said. "If they got him from behind like this the force of the blow should have thrown him down. He's been frisked, I think."

"Frisked?" I knew the word but it sounded strange coming from Biff.

"I mean that someone rolled him over to look through his pockets. See? This one is still turned inside out like."

"Don't touch him," I said, thinking more about the blood than the sheriff.

"No, honey, I won't. You've done enough of that for all of us. What did ya do, fall over him?"

Biff didn't wait for me to answer. He took the flashlight from me again and let it play around the surrounding ground. As the light traveled I could see where I had made my mistake. Instead of turning a little to the right when I left the office, I must have turned left. Biff found a cleared space a few feet from the body. He put down his coat for me to sit on. Then he lit two cigarettes. We didn't speak until Mandy came back. We could hear him whistling loudly. Then he sat down beside me. He was out of breath and beads of sweat were on his forehead.

"I got the sheriff and the doctor," he said after a moment's rest. "I called the saloon, too. They'll wonder why we're late for the show. I just told 'em we had an accident. I thought it was better not to let this thing out until the sheriff takes a look."

"My boy," Biff said, "you are getting to be a cop's delight."

"I broke in the act already," Mandy replied. "One more corpse and I'm ready for the big time."

We sat silently until we saw the headlights and heard the car drive up. The sheriff and the others gathered around what was left of Cliff Corny Cobb. Biff showed them the pocket that had been turned inside out. He explained how I had touched the body.

"Were you three together?" the sheriff asked casually.

I thought Biff hesitated before answering. "No," he said finally. "Mandy and I separated a while back. We were looking for Evangie, and Gyp here went to telephone and got lost. I heard her screaming, guess Mandy did too, so we just followed her voice."

"That's about right," Mandy said.

The doctor looked up from the body. He seemed to be puzzled about something.

"When did you start all this traipsing around?" the sheriff asked. He had seen the doctor's expression and must have recognized it.

"Not more than a few minutes," Biff said.

The sheriff smiled at the doctor.

"Well, let's get him out of here and let's get these people together again. I left Evangie—your mother—at the trailer. The two gals were locked in separate rooms there, like they were afraid of each other. You must have all had quite a time of it. That Dimples one was having hysterics. The Gee Gee Graham girl had to almost break down the door to get at her. Did someone tell 'em about this, or did they just get an idea that something was wrong?"

The sheriff spoke casually but he kept his eyes on my face.

"Dimples was afraid that something had happened to Mother," I said. "She'd been gone so long, and then we realized how long Corny had been gone and she . . ."

"She thought your mother might have killed him . . ."

"Oh, no," I said quickly. "It was the other way around. She thought maybe Corny had—that's why I telephoned the doctor."

As we walked toward the trailer Biff told the sheriff about the four thousand dollars. The men had put the body in the back of our car and had driven away with it. The sheriff was alone with us. He took the money from Biff and put it into his pocket. Then he took out his gun and kept it in his hand until we were in the trailer.

Mother was the only one who was composed. She sat on the daybed, sipping a hot toddy. "All this excitement," she said. "Just because I was away for a few hours."

I knew she was pleased, but Dimples lifted her swollen face as Mother spoke. She shoved a strand of hair from her bloodshot eyes and stared at the sheriff.

"Something's happened," she said. Her voice sounded as though there might be a cord around her neck choking her.

Her hands gripped the arms of the chair as she leaned forward. "What is it?" Dimples asked. "What's happened?"

Gee Gee pushed her gently back into the chair.

"Biff said he was going to call the sheriff," Gee Gee said. "Nothing else is going to happen, is it, Sheriff?"

The sheriff shook his head slowly.

"No, I don't think anything more could happen," he said. He watched Gee Gee massage Dimples's head for a moment. Then he looked at the bottle of rye on the stove.

"I brought it to them," Mother said. "When I stopped in to get the dogs' dinner. I don't approve of so much drinking but I felt an asthma attack coming on and hot toddys sometimes helps me." She smiled over her glass at the sheriff.

"Why did you lock yourself in the bedroom?" the sheriff asked suddenly. He watched Dimples as he spoke, watched her tremble and watched her hands go white from gripping the arms of the chair.

"I—was afraid," she said chokingly.

"How long were you in there?" he asked.

"I don't know. I don't know. I don't know anything. I just want to get out of here."

Dimples jumped to her feet and ran toward the door before the sheriff could grab her. He seized her shoulders and shook her.

"Look here now," he said roughly. "Cliff Corney Cobb was found stabbed in the back a few feet from here. Are you sure you didn't pretend to have hysterics so you could sneak out the back door and kill him?"

Dimples stared at the sheriff while he was talking. Her mouth fell open. Then suddenly a crafty smile made the sides of her mouth curl.

"I'm sure I didn't leave the trailer," she said slowly. Her narrowed eyes turned to Gee Gee. "But I can't swear that she didn't."

In a split second Gee Gee would have hit Dimples. Biff moved too quickly for her, though. He held her tightly while she let her arms flay about.

"Why don't you stop?" Biff said softly. "Can't you see they want you to do just what you're doing? As long as we stick together, they can't do a damn thing to us. We fall out and . . ."

"I can't help it," Gee Gee said. "She knows damn well I kept pounding on that door every minute she was in there. What in hell would I kill Corny for, anyway?"

Biff released hold on Gee Gee. He led her slowly but surely to the bedroom. As they passed the stove, Biff picked up the bottle.

Gee Gee relaxed. "It's O.K. now," she said. "I was just sore for a minute."

"I'm sorry, too," Dimples said. She relieved Biff of the bottle and poured out two drinks, one for Gee Gee.

Biff stood in the bedroom doorway and spoke softly to Hank. "I don't know much about the corpses, but I got an idea Corny's been dead for a couple hours, anyway. In fact, I got an idea he was killed while we were all together in the office,"

"What makes you think that?" the sheriff asked.

"Because of the five bucks for one thing. Dimples had just given it to him to buy a bottle. Seems to me he'da put it in his pocket if he'd had time. He wouldn't have loitered either, not with a fiver for a bottle in his hands. He never spent much time thinking that over. When he had the dough and the thirst he moved fast. Then I caught the look the doc here gave you when he was examining the body. He was telling you rigor mortis had set in, wasn't he?"

"The blood was fresh," I said.

"I got that figured out, too," Biff said with a careless wave of his hand. "I think you dislodged it when you tripped over the body. I took me a good look at the wound. There was congealed blood around it. That's one reason I didn't ask you right away if you'd killed him."

"Me?" I shrieked.

"Let's not go through all that again," Biff said impatiently. "Somebody killed him. It could have been you just as easy as anybody else."

The sheriff pulled out a chair and sank into it heavily.

"You're saving me a lot of breath," he said to Biff, "but if you don't mind, I'll do the questioning."

He turned to Mother and spoke more kindly. "What were you doing before you came to my office this afternoon?"

Mother looked down into her empty glass for a moment before answering.

"Well," she said slowly, "I'd had an asthma attack. After it cleared up we started out to visit a few people. We got as far as Mr. Hopkins's trailer, that's little Johnny's father, and then the car drove up and we got in and drove to town. That's all."

"We?" the sheriff asked.

"Mrs. Smith and me, of course. She had been helping me with my asthma attack."

"And the car? Who drove that?"

"Oh, the car." Mother seemed surprised that the sheriff didn't know about that. "It belonged to the insurance people, Mamie's insurance people. She had to go into town to sign some papers, and I went along for the ride. I don't trust those insurance people. I know all about them and I wanted to be there to see that Mamie got what was coming to her. You might say I went along for mercenary reasons."

"Did you go with her to the insurance man's office?' the sheriff asked.

"Oh, yes," Mother said. "But everything seemed to be all right. There were so many questions, though, and so many things to sign and everything. It was stuffy in the office, too, so I just thought I'd take a little walk. The office was quite close to yours, so I just dropped in to say hello."

The sheriff smiled. "I'm mighty glad you did," he said. "Then for all but the time you were in town Mamie Smith was with you, eh?"

Mother nodded yes.

Biff was busy heating water for another hot toddy. He took the potholder from the hook behind the stove and wrapped it around the handle of the pan. He placed a spoon in the glass with the liquor and sugar and added the water. Then he handed it to Mother.

"You say you were all together?" the sheriff said later to Biff. "When was that?"

"It was when Evangie was having her attack. We left for the office to have a drink and talk a little without her hear—without disturbing her."

"That was when Cliff Cobb left for the liquor, eh?"

No one answered him.

"Well, that sort of changes the complexion of things then," he said. "I'm not sure when he was stabbed, but I know it wasn't recently. Within the last hour or so, that is. If you people can all vouch for each other it sort of lets you out."

His hands began unwrapping the money. He counted it carefully. Then he placed it on the stove top and looked more closely at the *Racing Form*. It had been torn in half, but the date line was still attached. I had noticed it before. Now I saw that Hank was interested in it.

"September fifth," he said. "That's only two days ago. You say it was in the closet, eh?"

Biff walked over and opened the closet door. He moved the clothes aside and showed the sheriff the empty knot-hole.

"It was rolled up in that hole," he said.

"Any idea who it belongs to?" the sheriff asked.

"Idea? Sure," Biff replied, "but I'm not going to tell you my ideas. Go get some of your own." He laughed a little self-consciously. Then he became serious.

"Wait a minute, Hank," he said. "I might as well tell you what I think. You can use it or toss it. We were looking for something, understand? The thing you asked us not to mention in front of Evangie. Well, first we looked through the pantry. Remember when Gyp said she thought there was somebody in the trailer while she was sleeping? I told you the pantry door was open, didn't I? Well, I got thinking. What if she interrupted someone when she woke up? Someone who was hiding some-thing in the pantry? So I took a good look. I dumped out all the groceries and even pulled the innards out of a loaf of bread. I didn't find a thing. If someone had been hiding something, it's a cinch they didn't hide it in the pantry.

"Then I thought maybe they had been taking something out of the pantry. In the meantime we started searching the trailer. We tore the place apart. We didn't find what we were looking for, but we did find that wad of money. Naturally, I decided that whoever had the stuff had sold it. They were afraid to flash the roll, so they hid it. That's my idea. I got another, but for the time being I'm keeping it to myself."

Hank didn't have a chance to coax Biff for the other idea. Mother had suddenly decided to ask what it was that was being kept a secret from her. She asked rather loudly, too, and very firmly.

"It's all over now, so why let yourself get upset?" the sheriff asked.

Mother wanted to be the judge as to what was upsetting. That was obvious, so the sheriff told her the truth.

"It was hashish, I think, a form of dope," he said wearily. "But you didn't get enough to make . . ."

Mother thought over the word hashish. I could see her mouth form the pronunciation. Her hands began to tremble and her face turned white, a chalk white.

"You mean I'm a cocoon sniffer?" she asked.

Gee Gee laughed. She should have, because Mother really played the scene well. She was deserving of more than laughter, and I told Gee Gee so.

"That's all right, Louise," Mother said, pulling herself up from the chair. "I would expect something like that from anyone as inconsiderate as Gee Gee." Mother went to the door and opened it. 'If you'll fix my bed, Biff, I'll retire."

Mother let her eyes stray around the room. She was unsmiling. No one was going to laugh on her exit line, and Mother knew it.

"You can stay, Louise, if you wish, but I find the company very uncongenial."

21 BIFF LOOKED AT HIS WATCH. IT WAS TWO-thirty. I could hear the even breathing of sleeping people coming from the trailer. Mandy was in the bedroom. Mother was in the car, and the two girls were in the living room. They had been asleep for hours, it seemed. Really, it was less than that.

"Do you think something could have happened to Mamie?" I whispered to Biff.

He shrugged his shoulders. Then he lifted the glass to his lips and drank. We were on our second bottle of Old Grandad, but I couldn't even get a glow. It might have been the humidity that kept me from feeling gay. Maybe it was a case of the nerves.

"She might have eloped with the insurance man," Biff said seriously. "Or maybe she's filling in at the saloon for Dimples."

I was certain that the rye wasn't wasted on Biff, anyway. But he didn't look drunk. Every now and then he would sit forward in the camp chair as though he heard something. He had turned down the gaslight and we were sitting in the shadow under the lean-to. Mosquitoes and gnats swarmed around the lamp. The odor of rye and citronella filled the air.

"I think we'll be able to get away from here tomorrow," Biff said suddenly.

"Sure, honey."

"I mean it," Biff said. "The hitch should be finished by now. I think it's been fixed since yesterday. Hank just wanted to make sure we'd hang around."

"And now it's fixed we just jump in the car and drive away, huh? Just leave the bodies in the morgue, don't bother waiting for the inquest, forget all about a trial and everything."

"The inquest is at nine in the morning. By two we ought to be loaded and on our way." Biff leaned back his chair and braced his feet on the rickety table. "You see, I'm going to give the sheriff his murderer. I thought I'd wait and spring it during the inquest. That gives me a little time to get some facts together."

Now, I would never have married Biff if I hadn't had a feeling of affection for him. I had known him for years and we always had fun together. I laughed at most of his jokes because they amused me. I liked the way his eyes twinkled when he looked at me. Being married to him gave me a sense of security I had never known. I usually respected his judgment, but at that moment I wondered if any of those things really mattered.

"Look, funny man," I said. "I want you to know that from this minute on the honeymoon is over. You are going on the wagon. You aren't even going to get a chance to feel the outside of a beer bottle. What drinking there is to be done in our little family will be handled very nicely by me."

I shoved the cork in the Granddad bottle and put it on the ground next to my chair.

"I suppose you think I don't know who the murderer is?" Biff said. "Well, at that rate, my pretty, unsullied bride, you have a bit of a surprise coming to you. Want to play a game, a game of guess who?"

"No."

"All right then," Biff said. "Now, this is how we play it. You ask me twenty questions and I answer 'yes' or 'no' to 'em. Like for instance I was thinking about Joe Doaks. You ask me, 'Is he living?' and I say, 'Yes' again. That goes on until you use up your twenty questions. If you don't guess him you lose. If you lose, you go on the wagon, and what drinking there is to be done in our little family will be handled very nicely by me."

"I'm going to bed," I said, rising to my feet with great dignity. Then I remembered I had no bed to go to. So I sat down again.

"Is it a man?" I asked.

"Yep," Biff said, grinning at me.

"Is he from one of the five leading countries?"

"Yep."

"Living?"

"Yep."

"Please answer 'yes' or 'no,'" I said frigidly. "That yep business makes you sound like an acrobat getting ready to leap."

Biff's grin stretched into a broad smile. "Look, Punkin," he said. "I'll give you a hint. One of the answers is a saloon keeper with ideas that he oughta carve a niche for himself in show business."

Biff leaned back in the chair and made a tent with his hands. He was quite pleased with himself.

"That's all, brother," I said. "If you're going to get up on a stand tomorrow morning and say that Cullucio murdered all three of those guys, you are going to attend the inquest without me. I won't sit around while you make a damn fool of yourself. How, for instance, are you going to explain how he murdered the guy in San Diego?"

"Who said anything about murder?" Biff said. It was obvious that I had insulted him by even suggesting such a thing. Not only insulted him, but hurt his feelings, too. "We were just playing an innocent little game," he said. "Right away you have to talk about murders. Ghoulish, I'd say if anybody asked me."

"Nobody asked you, so why don't . . ."

Biff had turned off the lamp. With a quick motion he jumped to his feet. I heard the chair as it was turned over. Then I felt his hands on my shoulders.

"Duck!" he whispered hoarsely.

I fell to my knees and Biff rolled me under the trailer. My head hit the steps with a thud, but Biff kept pushing me until I could feel the wheels pressing against my arm. Then he was beside me breathing heavily.

"Look, Joe," I said, "if you want a drink, ask for it. You don't have to go through all this for . . ."

He put his hand against my mouth. At least I thought he meant my mouth. In the darkness it was closer to my ear, but I suddenly got the hint that he wasn't clowning.

Then I heard the footsteps. Someone was tiptoeing through the grass. They were walking toward our trailer. Biff fumbled for something in his pocket. I felt the chill steel of a gun. I heard the dull click of the safety catch being released. Biff's hand, holding the gun, trembled.

I heard someone whisper his name, "Biff?"

It was a woman's voice.

Biff let his breath out in a deep sigh of relief. "O.K.," he said quietly.

He rolled out from under the trailer leaving me there alone. He moved toward the table and scratched a match. Then he lit the lamp. I saw the silver dancing shoes with the run down heels first. They were dusty, the bare legs above them were scratched and bleeding.

"Thank Gawd you're here," the female voice mumbled. The feet moved over to the chair, and I heard the canvas creak as the weight of a body stretched it. Biff's hand reached for the bottle near the chair, but not quickly enough.

Bottle and all I rolled out from under the trailer. Before I got to my feet I greeted my friend Joyce Janice.

"It's so nice of you to drop in on us," I said. "Biff and I were thinking of fixing up a little guest room under the trailer. It's so cozy down there."

Biff didn't seem to think that was funny. He snatched the bottle from my hand and pulled out the cork. Then he handed it to Joyce and watched her while she gulped it down.

Unaided I scrambled to my feet. When I got my first good look at Joyce I suddenly knew why Biff thought she needed a drink.

Her dress was ripped up the side, showing her naked, scratched leg. Her arms were cut and bleeding from her wrists to her shoulders. Her makeup was smeared over her sweaty face. She was terrified.

"Get some hot water," Biff said.

Without thinking about waking the sleepers, I ran into the trailer and lit the stove. I pumped some water into a pan and put it over the flame. Then I grabbed a clean towel and a bottle of iodine from the drug shelf. Dimples mumbled in her sleep. Then she rolled over and was quiet.

Gee Gee sat up from her floor bed and yawned loudly. "Wassa matter?" she asked.

"Bring out the water when it gets hot," I said. I stepped over her and went outside again.

"I'm all right," Joyce said weakly. "I just ran so fast that I must have scratched myself on the bushes or something."

She swayed dizzily, and Biff made a motion to hold her. I got there first. The shock of seeing a half-naked woman coming out of the darkness was wearing off, and if there was any holding necessary I intended to do it. Not only that, but I had an idea Biff had almost expected a visitor and I didn't like it.

Gee Gee stumbled down the trailer steps with the pan of water. She looked at Joyce and put the water on the table calmly. Then she stopped short and looked again.

"What the hell's this?" she said.

"Close your mouth, dear," I said slowly. "Miss Janice has been running through the bushes. She was so anxious to get here she couldn't wait for the streetcar."

I dipped the towel into the water and began washing off the dust and blood from her shoulder. She winced a little from pain.

"These don't look like bush scratches to me," I said. One of the scratches was deep, as though a knife had slashed the flesh. I patted the wound more carefully.

"Get Mandy up," I said to Gee Gee. "Tell him to call Dr. Gonzales and tell him to bring whatever he needs to sew up knife wounds."

Joyce had fainted.

"Poor kid," Biff said as we carried her into the trailer.

Mandy threw back the sheet from his bed and put the pillow under Joyce's tousled head. He snatched up a pair of trousers from the chair and began stepping into them as he ran toward the office.

"She was trying to help me," Biff said. He rubbed her wrist being careful to avoid the cuts, and in a minute she opened her eyes.

"They've got her in the back room . . ." she said. "I tried to listen like you told me, but I couldn't hear everything. She was crying and screaming like a crazy woman. She kept saying, 'You did it, you dirty dog.' Then I'd hear a slap and a muffled scream. She said, 'You can't get away with it, and things like that. I—I was standing near the door. It was dark. I didn't think they could see me, but suddenly the door opened and something hit me . . ."

Joyce put her hand to her head. Then she pulled it away quickly. There was a blue bump on her forehead. She moaned softly when I patted it with the hot cloth.

"I ran as fast and I could and when I rushed out of the place I felt the hot sting in my arm. If I hadn't been running the knife maybe would have killed me."

She looked up at Biff and started to cry. Not a real cry, but like a hurt child, a small choking whimper.

"They tried to kill me, too," she sobbed. "I—I think they've already killed her . . ."

Joyce trembled violently for a second. Then she grabbed my hand tightly. She tried to say something, but nothing like words came out, just a frightened little gurgle and she was still again.

I spoke to Biff. "Is it Mamie now?"

Biff, looking down at Joyce, shrugged his shoulders. He touched her forehead gently.

"She'll be all right," he said. "It's more fright than anything. Poor kid, she must have run all the way here. Get those clothes off her, Punkin. When Mandy gets back, lock the door and don't open it unless you hear my voice. That means don't open it for *anybody* but me. I've work to do and it might take me a little while."

He dropped the gun on the dresser and opened the door. As an afterthought he kissed me on the nose. Then he was gone.

"Biff!" I ran to the door and threw it open.

My only answer was the loud knock of the truck motor turning over.

22 BEFORE GEE GEE COULD LOCK THE DOOR, Mother hurried into the trailer. She was barefoot and wild eyed. Her Life Everlasting was clutched in her hand.

"Well," she said, "I just heard Biff leave. I also heard what he said. Lock the door and don't open it for anyone! Indeed!

And what about me out there alone in the car? Am I to be bait for the murderer? Are you deliberately trying . . ."

"Mother, you know better than that. We naturally thought you had the car locked." I put my arms around her shoulders and led her toward the bed. Dimples was sleeping soundly, so I rolled her close to the wall and made room for Mother to lie down.

"You sleep here," I said, and Mother allowed herself to be tucked in.

"Turn off the light, Louise," Mother said plaintively. "It hurts my eyes."

I not only tuned off the light; I closed the door leading to the bedroom. Mother hadn't noticed Joyce and, under the circumstances, I was just as pleased. Then I locked the outside door and propped a chair under the knob and picked up the gun Biff had left for us. It was a large gun and it looked like an old one. I had never seen it before. I held it by the barrel because I was afraid of it.

"Put it down, honey," Gee Gee said. "You've got the business end pointing straight at me, and besides, remember the old gag. 'I didn't know it was loaded?'"

I placed the gun on the dresser. Oil from it had stained my hand, and I picked up a towel to wipe it off. Joyce began rolling and tossing on the bed and the motion started the flow of blood again. While Gee Gee and I were making up our minds what to do, Dimples burst into the room.

Her hair was rolled up in tin curlers and she wore the pink chin strap. Her puffy eyes were almost closed with sleep, but when she saw Joyce they popped open. She opened her mouth to scream. Suddenly she closed it.

"Well for Gawd's sake," she said impatiently. "Don't just stand there and watch her bleed to death. Do something!"

She didn't wait for us to react. She grabbed the towel from my hands and began tearing it into strips. The towel was strong and she tore it with her teeth. Even after Gee Gee offered her a pair of scissors, Dimples kept biting the hem of the coarse linen, then tearing it down. She snatched up a hair brush from the dresser and pushed me aside.

"You gotta help me now," she said. She tied the linen strips under Joyce's shoulder. She twisted it until Joyce's hand and arm turned white.

Joyce moaned, but Dimples twisted the brush even tighter.

"Hold this tourniquet," Dimples said to me, and, as Joyce opened her eyes, "Get her a drink."

The cool efficiency hardly matched her tousled hair and chin-strapped face. The marabou-trimmed kimono was a far cry from a crisp uniform, but Dimples's hand was steady when she poured the drink for Joyce. She lifted her carefully and held the glass to her lips.

Joyce drank part of the liquor. The rest trickled down her chin, and Dimples brushed it away gently. Then she let Joyce lie back on the pillow.

Dimples tipped the bottle to her mouth and took a long drink.

"Did you get a load of me?" she asked, wiping her mouth with the back of her hand. "Me, Dimples Darling, making like Florence Nightingale. Boy, I wish somebody'd taken a picture of it." Her eyes settled on Joyce. The laughter in them was gone. "Did they get the guy who done this?" she asked.

Gee Gee shook her head. "Biff's gone to the saloon. They got Mamie there."

Dimples looked at me.

"It's true," I said. "Joyce said so a minute ago. She said they almost got her, too."

"Almost!" Dimples said loudly. "What do you call that?" she asked, pointing to Joyce's arm. "But what the hell do they want with Mamie? Of all the unhep dames, she is it. Why that poor, old . . ."

"Shh . . ." Gee Gee grabbed Dimples's hand. "Did you hear something?"

It was a car stopping in front of the trailer. The door was slammed loudly. Then there was a sharp knock on the trailer.

"This is Dr. Gonzales," a voice said. "Open the door."

The handle was turned roughly. Then Mandy called in to us. "Come on, open up. The doc just got here."

I turned the key in the lock before I remembered Biff's warning. Gee Gee must have thought of it just as I did because she pushed me aside and relocked the door. She pressed her back against it and held her hands to her chest. Her eyes were frightened.

"Biff said not to open it for anyone . . ." she murmured.

Then I remembered the car leaving the driveway, Cullucio and the doctor together late at night. I thought of the room where Mother sat and played cards, the expensive books, the leather furniture. It wasn't the house of a small-town doctor. The draperies alone were worth more than that kind of a doctor could make in a year.

"Let 'em in, you dopes." Dimples looked at Gee Gee and me as though we had gone mad. "You want that poor kid to die with a doctor standing right outside? Get away from that door."

Gee Gee shook her head wildly. "He could have done it easy," she said. "He was with us in San Diego. He's been around every time anything's happened. He could even have done this to Joyce. How do we know where he's been for the last half hour?"

I suddenly realized she meant Mandy Hill! Not Dr. Gonzales, but *Mandy*. She was right, too. He could have . . .

"Get my asthma powder, please." Mother stood in the doorway between the two rooms. She held her robe tightly to her throat. Her breathing was heavy and uneven. She didn't see Joyce. "Hurry, Louise—bad attack . . ."

The Life Everlasting was on the stove. I poured a mound of it into the container top and gave Mother a towel for her head. Then I lit the powder. Mother sank weakly into a chair and buried her face under the towel. Her shoulders heaved spasmodically as she tried to get her breath. Her bare feet and ankles were moist with perspiration.

"Let me in there at once!" the doctor shouted angrily. He began pounding on the door with his fists. "This man tells me a woman's been injured. I demand that you open this door."

The pounding stopped. For a moment there was a silence. Then he was at the window. He tapped on it with a cane or something. The noise rang through the trailer. That window was bolted but the others at the back of the trailer were not only unlocked, they were open.

Mandy called to me from the back window of the living room. I could see the bushy hair as he stood on tiptoe to peer into the trailer. "Have you dames gone nuts or something?"

Then Gee Gee turned off the lights. "We're a solid target here," she said softly. "Lock those windows, Gyp. I wouldn't let them in if they showed me a badge from LaGuardia himself."

I almost touched Mandy's face as I slammed down the window and bolted it. Then I ran to the other two and locked them. Even before the last one was secured, I knew we were going to suffocate. Mother's asthma powder burned black and heavy, the air was thick with the smoke. It choked me and made my eyes tear.

"I'm leaving for Ysleta," the doctor said. His voice was steady with fury. "I'm returning with the sheriff, and you can do your explaining to him. If that woman dies, it will be criminal negligence on the part of each and every one of you."

The car started up, and Mandy screamed, "Hey, wait for me! I don't want to stay here alone with those dames. They blowed their tops. I'm scared to death of 'em."

I heard him walk around to the front of the trailer, then silence. I felt around in the dark for the bed. Then I sat on the edge of it. Mother's wheezing was the only sound in the trailer, the only sound in the night. I smelled Dimples's cloying perfume as she sat down next to me.

"Where in hell is this damned business going to end?" she said. "Here we are, cooped up in this trailer with Mandy outside alone. We leave him out there because we think he's the murderer, but what's to stop him from thinking the same about one of us? Gee Gee, for instance, could be the murderer for all I know. Or Joyce. She could have stabbed herself or something to throw suspicion away from him. Biff even, or Evangie, or you . . ."

"Or you," I said slowly.

Dimples waited a moment before she spoke. Her voice was husky when she said, "Sure, even me."

The rain fell softly at first, then it pounded on the trailer roof like buckshot. Gee Gee went to the back window and unlocked it.

"I can't stand it any longer," she said irritably. "If I gotta go, I don't want it to be by smothering to death. Anyway, if we can't handle one murderer between all of us and a gun, we deserve to get knocked off."

No one tried to stop her as she opened the window. The gust of air and rain that poured through the trailer was more important at that moment than all the murderers in the world. I fumbled for the matches and lit the lamp. Then I turned on the lights.

In the yellow glow I saw Mandy's fuzzy head framed in the open window. The rain made his hair kinkier, and it stood up straight from his forehead. The window sill covered all his face, all but the eyes; they were wide and staring. Staring at Dimples.

She held the gun in her hand. Not as I had held it, but the right way, and she had it pointed straight at Mandy.

"Don't move," she said evenly.

Mandy didn't move. His mouth sagged a little, otherwise he was motionless. Dimples didn't take her eyes from the open window. "Open that door, Gyp," she snapped. "I want to talk over a few things with this guy."

I didn't move. I couldn't.

Dimples's steady hand on the gun was wet with sweat. Her eyes had become pin points. "Let him in," she said.

Then Mandy moved. His head disappeared, and there was a scurry of feet and a sloshing sound of his shoes sliding through the fresh mud.

Dimples turned to the door and threw it open. "Get in here, you," she shouted.

"The hell I will," Mandy screamed. His voice sounded far away.

Dimples stood swearing into the darkness through the open

doorway with the rain beating against her thin kimono. The marabou clung wetly to her white cheeks, splotches of bluish red stained her neck and began traveling up her face. She swallowed painfully. Then her chin shook. The strap fell loose and the gun dropped from her fingers. A second later she followed the gun. Her body made a soggy noise as it sank to the floor. She looked soggy, too, as she lay there.

Gee Gee and I lifted her onto the daybed, and Mother poured out some water. The monkey, in his cage at the foot of the bed, grabbed out at Dimples's kimono and Mother slapped his hand. He shrieked with anger. Then the dogs began barking. Mother ignored them as she poured the water on Dimples's face.

"She just fainted," Mother said.

Gee Gee lifted Dimples's head and opened her eye gently. The pupil was gone. Nothing showed but a white round thing; white with thin veins of red lining it. Gee Gee looked up at Mother, then at me.

"I think she's been doped or something," she said hoarsely.

The dogs stopped barking as though they knew what Gee Gee had said. Bill's ears dropped and he slunk away.

"Look at how strained her face is," Gee Gee said. "Look at that funny color around her neck. Fainting doesn't do that."

Mother looked down at Dimples. Her asthma attack was wearing away, but she still breathed heavily.

"Who could have doped her though?" she said almost to herself. "She didn't eat anything we didn't eat. She didn't drink anything but that liquor . . ."

Dimples opened her eyes. "Gimme a drink," she said faintly.

"That's the wrong dialogue," Gee Gee said. "You shoulda said, 'Where am I?'"

Dimples tried to sit up. Then she fell back on the pillow. "Look I paid five bucks for a bottle," she complained weakly. "Just because the guy didn't deliver it is no reason my intentions weren't right."

By the time Gee Gee had poured out the water, Dimples was in another coma. Saliva dripped from the side of her mouth, and Gee Gee wiped it away with a Kleenex.

"Do you feel all right, Gyp?" Gee Gee asked a moment later.

"I think so," I said. "The air was making me dizzy for awhile, but I feel better now. Why?"

"Because I felt funny, too," Gee Gee said, "You know, Gyp, I think that liquor was doped!"

I was too surprised to hear the car drive up. The first I knew about it was when Biff burst into the room.

"Hey, I thought I told you to keep this door locked," he said. He wasn't angry, though. I knew why when I saw the familiar bulge of a bottle in his hip pocket. He started for the bedroom. Then he saw Dimples. She was still unconscious.

Dr. Gonzales followed Biff into the trailer. He leaned over Dimples and, taking her wrist in his hand, waited quietly for a second. Then he looked up.

"What's the meaning of this?" he said.

Gee Gee shrugged her shoulders helplessly. "Don't ask me," she said. "All of a sudden she just konked off, funnylike. Gyp and I carried her over to the bed and after awhile she came to, then she went out again. I thought maybe she'd been doped."

"What made you think that?" the doctor asked.

"Well, Gyp felt dizzy and I felt sorta funny, too, not so much dizzy as silly. My hands got numblike, and I saw things. Then, when I lifted Dimples's eyelid and saw the whiteness, I was pretty sure."

Dimples opened her eyes then. She raised herself up on her elbow and stared outside the room. "What hit me?" she said. "I can't get my breath. I'm all choked up . . ."

Mother went into action. She grabbed the box of Life Ever-lasting and poured a mound in the container top.

"Here, this will fix that. It makes my head clear right away . . ."

Mother touched a match to the powder and waited for the flame to die down before she reached for the towel.

Biff had been watching her. His mouth fell open and he pounded his fist on the stove top.

"That's it!" he shouted. "Why didn't I think of it before? Of course that's the best place in the world to hide it!"

Biff snatched the asthma powder from Mother and shoved it toward the doctor.

"Can you tell what's mixed up in this stuff?" he asked. "I mean can you tell if it's all asthma powder or if something else is in it?"

The doctor took the container from Biff and put it into his pocket. "I'll have to analyze it," he said.

"The hell you do," Biff said quickly. "I see it all now. Every time Evangie had an attack she inhaled it, she went a little nuts. It was the logical place to hide the dope. Nobody would think to look through a can of asthma powder for another kind of powder. Why I didn't think of it before is beyond me."

"You think that's what happened to me?" Dimples asked.

"Sure," Biff said with assurance. "I smelled the stuff the second I walked into the trailer. You must have gotten a couple good whiffs and, in your weakened, high-strung condition, you were just ripe for it."

Dimples liked the remarks about her condition.

"Matter of fact," she said, "I am run-down . . ."

She would have gone through a list of ailments if Biff and the doctor hadn't left to see Joyce. Gee Gee waited until they closed the door. Then she eyed the bottle.

"You know," she said, "even now, when I knew there's no dope in that rye, I still don't want a drink. I can't understand it, I don't want a drink!"

"Maybe you're cured of the habit," Mother said. "My sister married a man who took the Keeley cure, and believe it or not . . ."

Biff opened the bedroom door and came into the sitting room.

"Is Joyce all right?" Gee Gee asked.

Biff nodded. "Yeah, it's only a scratch. She bled a lot and she'll be a little weak for a while, but the doc's taking her into town so she'll get some rest. He just gave her a shot of something now to make her sleep, an opiate."

The doctor called to Biff. "Put on some water to boil. I have to clean this up a bit."

We crowded around the door as the doctor spoke.

"Are you positive she's all right?" Dimples asked.

"Positive," the doctor replied. "This won't even leave a scar."

Joyce stirred. She opened her eyes and stared at the doctor.

"Honest to Gawd?" she asked.

Opiate or no opiate, I thought, when you mention scars to strip teasers, they all come to.

"Honest," the doctor said softly.

Joyce fell back on the pillow with a happy smile on her face.

23

BIFF CLOSED THE BEDROOM DOOR. WITH A contented sigh he settled into the most comfortable chair in the trailer. Not because he was selfish, but because he was the man of the house and he wanted to look it. He wanted his womenfolk sitting around waiting patiently for the words to fall. His picture would have been complete had one of us placed his slippers at his feet.

Gee Gee climbed over his stretched-out legs and found a place on the bed next to Dimples. Mother, still a little wheezy, sat stiffly in a chair near the door. I stood beside the stove. Not because the bottle was there, but because I wasn't in a sitting mood.

Our man of the house, being a comic, took his own sweet time in getting to the point. He pulled a cigar from his pocket and smelled it lovingly. As though that wasn't bad enough, he had to touch a match to it.

"White Owl," he said comfortably. "Smell the feathers burning?"

We laughed politely. It was an effort, but we made it. Then there was another long silence.

"Would you like a little entrance music?" I asked finally. "Maybe eight bars of "Happy Days Are Here Again," as played on a comb?"

Silence. Nothing but the odor of burning feathers and Mother's wheezing to fill the air.

"Perhaps you'd rather go into the act cold?"

"If," Biff said with Theatre Guild enunciation, "you will allow everything in its chronological order and not make with the throat, I will name for you the murderer."

Naturally I was insulted. The offstage dialogue about my throat had become a bit tiresome during the past few days. Biff was rather overdoing the act of Provider, too. But I was more curious than insulted, so I kept quiet. I did kick off my shoes, light a cigarette, and pour myself a drink. It was obvious that we were in for a session.

Biff began modestly enough: "I don't know if you gals know just what kind of mental guy is sitting here talking to you. You got me pegged as a funny man. A man who makes with the stale jokes. What you overlook is that I am a guy who just found himself a murderer. I mean a murderer of the first water. Not somebody who lost their temper and skewered with an ice pick. Not a murderer who didn't-know-it-was-loaded, but a scheming, conniving murderer. I am not one to brag, but, I, Biff Brannigan, alone, unabetted, unaided, in fact, hampered by the police, have solved the case of Evangie's body!"

"My body!" Mother shrieked. "I'll have you remember that I had absolutely nothing to do with that corpse. Nothing besides burying it and that is what any mother would have done. Any mother with true feelings. Any mother with a grain of love for her daughter."

Mother had risen to her feet on that speech, and as she stood, one hand pressing against the side of the trailer, the other over her heart, she looked a little like Joan of Arc. She knew it too. She glanced around to see if the girls could get a good view. They could. Mother lapsed into an asthmatic satisfied silence.

"Yes," Biff said above the wheezing, "I know the murderer of a man named Gus. The murderer of Corny. The murderer of the second body. His name was Jones, incidentally. Ain't that a hellova name for a corpse? Jones! If you saw it on a hotel register you'd swear it was a gag. Mr. and Mrs. Jones—"

"I knew a Mr. and Mrs. Jones once," Mother said. "They lived next door to us in Seattle. He was a railroad man. A conductor on the Yessler Way cable car. His wife was a funny little woman, too. Three children, or was it four? I sort of remember a boy—Joe, no I think it was George—"

"I know all of this because of a little brush fire," Biff said when Mother stopped to think of the Jones's first names. "Everybody saw that fire. They could be in my shoes right this minute, but no! It was left to me, a burlesque comic—"

"And not too comical at this sitting," Gee Gee said. "The only funny thing is the gag about the shoes. Who in the hell'd want to be in those Juliets?"

"If you will leave my sartorial effects out of this I will go on," Biff said. "That is if you don't mind too kindly."

Biff wasn't annoyed, but I could see that one more crack would do it. I couldn't control Mother but I did give Gee Gee the eye. Biff waited until the eye talk was over.

"Yep, it was left to a comic to discover the weak point in an otherwise clever scheme to rob, plunder, kill, murder—"

"Nuts!" Gee Gee said. She reached for the bottle and tilted it to her lips. She gulped it daintily.

"You'll never be able to top the opening of this dialogue brother," she said. "Are you going to get to the blackout or is to be continued in this theater next week? Here we sit, the four of us, waiting for you to tell us something, and all you do is make words. Put 'em together! Answer me one quick question: have they got Cullucio? Yes or no? No gestures, no buildup, just a nice short yes or no!"

"Yes," he said. "Yes, they got him. But first I would like to tell you how and why. I will have to go back—"

"I wish to hell you'd go way back," Gee Gee muttered.

"As I said, I will have to go back to an afternoon in San Diego. Back to the afternoon when Evangie stopped in a drug-store and bought six cans of Life Everlasting. Had she bought one can this might never have happened to us. We all know that the murderer knew the heroin was in an asthma powder can. We all know about the two men who followed Evangie. We all know why Corny met his death. We all know why Joyce was stabbed—"

"You mean *you know*!" Gee Gee said. "So far all we know is that you have a big mouth. What about Corny and Joyce? What about those two guys following Evangie? What about the asthma powder? And what about that handkerchief found in the grave? What about the fire that set your nimble brain galloping along?

Biff twined his fingers around his suspenders, the red ones with FIREMAN printed on them, and leaned back in his chair.

"I have been in Ysleta a couple of hours while you dames were scaring the hell out of each other. In that time I found the answer to everything. Corny was killed because he sold information. He told the murderer the heroin was hidden in the asthma powder. He knew that because he saw Gus put it there in San Diego. He expected Gus to come around for it and he figured to cut himself in for a little dough when Gus appeared. But no Gus. Why? Because Gus was dead. But Corny does see someone prowling around the trailer. He knows what they're after and because there was no way he could sell the dope he tells 'em, for dough, of course, where to look. They look all right but they get the wrong container. They go to Corny with a beef. He says for them to take it easy or he'll tell what he knows about the body in the woods. You see, he didn't see Evangie bury the body. He saw the second body being buried! He saw Evangie on her way *out* of the woods. He thought she had hidden the heroin. Not that it mattered to him, he had four thousand-some-odd bucks salted away in the trailer. He didn't give a damn who got the heroin so long as he had the money. Where he made his mistake is when he told the murderer he knew they had buried a body. That is when he signed his death warrant."

Biff paused long enough to let the garbled facts sink in, then a little longer while he poured a drink.

"What I like best," Gee Gee said, "is the 'signed-his-death-warrant' line. That is fancy dialogue. Who, may I ask, writes your material?"

"You think I'm wrong, eh?" Biff asked. "Well, then, I'll go on! Evangie's two beauty boys were Cullucio's men."

"No kidding?" Gee Gee said coldly.

"Sure, finding Jones's body scared hell out of 'em. See, Jones was one of Cullucio's waiters. They knew if Hank ever took a look at the corpse he'd recognize him right off the bat. They're the ones who bashed in his face and tore out the tailor label. They were protecting their boss, that's all."

Something had occurred to me! I was almost ashamed to mention it, but I felt it my duty, as wife, to tell.

"I should have known about the waiter," I said. Biff looked at me sharply.

"Cullucio told me he'd been gone a couple days, and I should have put two and two together, really. Only he was so calm about telling me. Just as though waiters are found dead in the woods every day. He said the guy had been missing and that was that."

"Cullucio would," Biff said laconically.

"Did they get those two guys too?" I asked.

Biff nodded, and I felt a sigh escape me. The only way I wanted to see them again was behind bars. There are muscle boys and there are muscle boys. Cullucio's were the type who look best in stripes. The thought of them following Mother, hiding around in the woods, sneaking through the trailer, made me tremble. The picture of Cullucio, sitting next to me in the saloon, didn't help my nerves either. I could see his white teeth gleaming, his dark hands with the tufts of hair growing on the knuckles, his way of dipping his cigar in his liquor before he smoked. My mouth started to shake. I couldn't make it stop. I couldn't rid myself of that mental picture.

"He—he—could have killed all of us," I finally managed to say.

"Yes, but he didn't, so calm down," Biff said. "He didn't kill anybody—"

"Hiring someone else to do it for him is just as bad," I said. "And if I want to have a case of mild hysterics I will thank you to mind your own business."

I had stopped trembling. I wasn't even frightened. I had just one emotion left. A slow, burning fury at the saloon keeper.

"For him to pick on us of all people," I said. "Dumping his old corpse in our trailer! He might have known it was my honeymoon!"

Biff was going to say something, but Dimples got in there first. She pulled the marabou-trimmed robe closer to her chest and adjusted her chin strap.

"I'll probably have a sweet time trying to collect my salary from The Happy Hour," she said. "It may be blood money, but I worked for it and I'd like to get it. I got a fiver coming to me from Corny, too. I guess that dough will go to the state or something. They'll find some way to stiff me. It's my usual luck, dammit. I get me a nice job, short hours, no matinees, I was going over swell, too, and the joint turns out to be a dope drop."

"Say, The Happy Hour isn't the only saloon in Ysleta, you know," Biff said. "They got enough of 'em in town that you could make a career from 'em. I could maybe make a deal for you at The Blinking Pup."

His voice sounded casual enough, but knowing Biff I looked at him closely. He had something on his mind, and I wasn't sure I was going to like it.

"Matter of fact," he said, "I thought you gals might feel a little squeamish about staying on at The Happy Hour."

"Squeamish," Dimples said. "If it means what I think it means, the word'll fit."

Biff said, "I was talking to a guy about it a few hours ago. He runs The Blinking Pup. Caught the act at The Happy Hour, and he thought you were pretty solid."

Dimples smiled as much as the chin strap would allow. "He did, huh?"

"Yep," Biff said, "he told me he could use Gee Gee too. Forty a week and meals. Four-week contract. That's not to be kicked around, you know. I could maybe get him to up the money a little."

Gee Gee and Dimples looked at each other, then at Biff.

"Can I maul it around in my head for a while?" Gee Gee asked.

"Sure," Biff said. A broad gesture went with the word. "Think it over. It sounds like a good bet to me, but after all, you're the girls to decide."

Then I got it! I might have guessed from Biff's expression, but being on the slow side that night it took me a little longer than usual. I knew then that when Biff let his eyes travel over the trailer he was mentally picturing it without Gee Gee and Dimples. He looked at Mother for a moment, then he shrugged his shoulders slightly.

"That one stopped you, didn't it?"I asked sweetly.

Biff started, then his face broke into a grin.

"Not exactly," he said pensively. "I got an idea on that score, too."

I was sure he had.

"And what about Mandy?" I asked. "Saloon or no saloon, it won't be easy to sell him as a single. And of course there's always Mamie. Have you got her all set as the Belle of The Blinking Pup?"

Gee Gee thought that was very funny. Biff didn't.

"I'm getting off the original script," he said. There's something I got to tell you all. It's about poor Mamie. She's—"

A car stopped in front of the trailer. The headlights glared from the window into Biff's face, and a second later someone pounded on the door. Mother quickly fluffed up her hair and pinched her cheeks until they were quite pink, then she opened the door for the sheriff.

We all faced him silently. He took off his hat and held it awkwardly in his large hands. He gave the impression of having to stoop a little so his head would clear the ceiling of the trailer. His high-heeled shoes looked silly. I suddenly saw him as a musical-comedy sheriff, and the idea wouldn't go away.

"I can see you all know," he said. He let his head drop for a moment, and it was as though the orchestra should go into a number at that point.

"Biff was just telling us about Mamie," Mother said. "He didn't get very far with it."

She realized too late that her words were hardly complimentary. As a quick cover-up she added, "Now that you're here maybe we can get a straight story."

The sheriff seated himself as close to Mother as he could. Biff offered him a drink and he refused it. His eyes were on the bedroom door. The knob turned and the door opened. I had forgotten about Gonzales. He turned down the lamp near the bed and picked up his black bag, then he walked on tiptoe to the door and closed it behind him. He stood within touching distance from me, and in the shadows his teeth, when he smiled at Hank, were white. Almost like phosphorus.

"I'll send the large car for Miss Janice," he said softly. "She'll be better off in town where I can keep an eye on her."

I watched him as he fastened his black bag. His long, dark fingers moved gracefully as he slipped the leather strap through the clasp. His head was bent over, and the light fell on the black oily hair. When he walked toward the outer door I felt a sudden urge to stop him. I couldn't explain it. I wanted to look at him closely for a moment. He asked Dimples how she felt.

"Like a babe," she said smiling up at him.

Then he was at the door; it opened and closed behind him. I heard the car start up, the gears meshed, I could hear the tires splashing through the soft mud. I ran to the window and looked out. A red taillight flicked for a moment, then it was gone, but not before I saw the light-colored roadster. It was a long, expensive-looking roadster. I had seen it before. It had left the doctor's driveway while Biff and I stood in the darkness. That night Cullucio was driving it.

24 "IT'S CULLUCIO!" MY VOICE SEEMED TO RING through the trailer. "I knew there was something about him that was familiar. Stop him! Stop him!"

Biff began shaking me. I could see Mother rushing around getting a glass of water for me. Dimples had jumped up from the bed and was running toward the window. Gee Gee held my arm when I tried to open the door. Their faces and their movements were like a kaleidoscope. Hank's face staring at me, Mother holding a glass to my lips. Biff's arms holding me.

"Leave me alone, please." I tried to push them away from me. "Don't you see it at all? Don't you realize we've never seen them together? His house, all those expensive things in it. That car! When I saw his hands, I knew it. The black tufts of hair growing on his knuckles. You gave him the can of asthma powder, too. He has it right now and he's gone!"

Biff was pushing me into the chair. No one made a move to stop Cullucio. They stared at me as though I had gone mad.

"Cullucio's in Ysleta," Hank said softly. "I just left him and I know. The doc—well—it's not supposed to be known, but the doc is his brother. I've known it all long, but there didn't seem any point in telling it around town. Doctors in a town like this have to have a certain dignity. It doesn't sound good to say his brother runs a saloon. Especially when they're partners in that saloon."

"But the names, Cullucio, Gonzales—"

"Those two names don't even scratch the surface. They have a dozen more, all legal too, if they want to sue them. That Gonzales in Mexico is like Smith in the states. Cullucio isn't even a Mexican name. The doc's all right though. I've known him since he first started practicing here. Cullucio's all right too, in his own way, of course. Honest as the day's long, but a funny sense of honesty—"

"Honest?" Gee Gee screamed. "What kind of people are these?" she looked wildly around the room. "Murderers, dope peddlers. Honest people yet!"

"Who said he was a murderer?" Hank asked

There was no answer.

"Who said he was a dope peddler?" Hank said.

Then Biff spoke: "They must have gathered it from what I was telling them. I never got to finish; they kept interrupting me all the time. I was telling them how I got suspicious when I saw the remains of the burned trailer, then I started from the beginning and—"

"Funny thing about the trailer," Hank said slowly. He pulled at his chin and nodded his head thoughtfully. "I should have seen it myself. Had my eye on this trailer camp for some months now, and I let a thing like that slip by."

Biff leaned back in his chair and looked at the ceiling. "Well," he said condescendingly, "we all can't see everything. Me, now, the second I look over the ground I know there's something funny going on. Trailer burned to a crisp, woods burned too, and still the grass around the trailer hasn't even been scorched. I don't pay much attention to the smell of gasoline around the fire, cars and all, bound to be a smell of gasoline, but no flying spark could burn that trailer the way it was burned. No, sir. Then her moving in with us so sudden like. Oh, I knew something was up all right. I just kept my eyes and ears open, and there it was. Plain as day. What a setup. Traveling around with a beauty shop. Covering all the border towns regularly. Having a couple guys in each town deliver the stuff she brought in, even looking like she does—"

"Damn shame you didn't think of those things before the other two guys got killed," Hank said. "If you'd come to me in the first place this might have had a different ending. People oughta realize that's what the law's for. Like with Cullucio. He could have told me how he suspected his waiter. I would have gotten some of the boys to look around. But no. He goes and sends for a couple of his own. They mash in the face so we can't identify the body. They know all along who's guilty but they don't give us credit for realizing it. That's just like a crook. They keep lying so much themselves they don't expect anybody'll ever believe 'em."

Gee Gee stood stage center with her hands on her hips. Her hair, I noticed, was beginning to turn a pale purple with a burnished effect at the part.

"Do you two baboons mean to sit there with your bare faces hanging out and tell me that Mamie Smith from Oologah murdered those men?"

"It's Watova," Biff said, "eight miles west of Oologah."

"Yes, she did it all right," Hank said.

Mother pushed Gee Gee away and took the floor.

"She couldn't have," Mother said. "I'm a judge of character and I know Mamie wouldn't do anything so—so—well, so ungenteel. Not only that, but Gus, or whatever his name was, was killed in San Diego. Mamie couldn't have killed him. Maybe the one named Jones, I don't care about that, but she couldn't have killed Corny either, because she was helping me with my asthma attack at the time."

"Evangie," Biff said softly. "Remember how Mamie arrived the same day we did? Well, she came from San Diego. She killed Gus there, because he was trying to open a branch office and cut her out with the guys who really controlled this ring. She expected to find the heroin on the body, but it was gone. She had seen him go into our trailer and she figures he has the stuff there, which he did, only he doesn't tell her where. She hides the corpse in our bathtub—"

"Why our bathtub?" Dimples asked. "I think that's damn inconsiderate of her."

"It was the first trailer near hers for one thing. Then, when she saw Gus in here, she thought he might be getting mixed up with us. She figured out the trailer business and she thought he was using ours, in cahoots with one of us—or all of us, for that matter—for the same purpose. She was almost sure of it when she saw Evangie bury the body that night. Then when Corny propositions her she thinks it is very nice indeed. Nothing like having a group of grifters falling out. It always leaves an empty spot for someone else, and Mamie had herself set up as that somebody else."

"Are you telling me that Mamie, my friend, thought I was mixed up in that dope business?" Mother said coldly.

"I think she thought so at first," Biff admitted. "But after she got to know you she couldn't have. She wanted to get rid of Corny as soon as he gave her the bum steer about the heroin. Her idea was to put the handkerchief in the grave and let Hank find it. Then in a sweet-old-ladylike way she was going to say that she 'thought' there was something wrong with Corny and 'admit' she saw him bury the body. After all, he was there, he saw her bury the body. She was just doing a switch, and it would be his word against hers. But the law's too slow. She can't wait. She knows she's dealing with a guy who wouldn't sit still for anything but dough and lots of it. And he's threatening. She waits until she has him alone, then she lets him take the knife in his back. She was with Evangie all right—that is, until Evangie gets the towel over her head. Then Mamie walks out quietly to the office and waits until Corny comes out. Zoop, it's over, she hotfoots it back to Evangie and asks her if she's feeling better. Naturally, Evangie thinks she's there all the time."

Mother listened to Biff. A frown creased her forehead.

"I can't believe it," she said. "I caught her going through the girls' things one day. I spoke to her, and she told me she would never do anything like that again. I knew she was a petty thief but I really thought I had made her see the light. She said she never had pretty things of her own and—"

"All she wanted," Biff said, "was the pretty heroin."

"Did she stab Joyce too?" Dimples asked.

"No," Biff said. "Cullucio's man did that. By mistake of course. He thought he was hitting Mamie, see; she was in the room talking to Cullucio. The 'boys' were right outside the door, still protecting their boss. Joyce is listening, like I asked her to, and she hears Mamie threaten Cullucio. He's scared to death anyway because of his dead waiter. When Mamie tells him that waiter was her man for Ysleta, he really goes wild. It's a wonder he didn't kill her himself. She's threatening to tell Hank, and Cullucio starts to struggle with her. That's when Joyce tries to run away. Cullucio's man thinks it's Mamie running down the hall so he grabs out at her——"

"Grabs out with a knife," Gee Gee said. "That's cute, too."

"Anyway," Biff went on, "when Joyce gets to the trailer and tells me about Mamie being at The Happy Hour I drive like hell to get there in time. Cullucio would have killed her in a minute if she ever tried to frame him. Not because of himself but because of his brother. That's what Hank means when he says Cullucio has a funny sense of honesty. He figures Mamie is a crook, his brother isn't. If it's a question of one or the other having to go, he's not going to waste time thinking over it. I made him understand that nothing could happen to Gonzales, and we called Hank to come over and pick up the dame."

"She was like a wild woman," Hank said. He looked down at the four deep scratches on his hand. "Boy, did she put up a fight."

"Well," Mother said, "I hardly blame her for that. Three of you picking on one woman. I think it's disgraceful. And now talking behind her back when she isn't here to defend herself."

"Defend herself?" Hank said. "Why she's a—"

Mother put up her hand. "Please," she said. "You've done quite enough. You don't have to become deleterious. I would rather you left us now, I want to be alone with my daughter."

The sheriff picked up his hat. He looked from Mother to Biff. Biff shrugged his shoulders again, this time hopelessly. The sheriff said goodbye to all of us, then he left.

Mother waited until she heard his car leave, then she turned to me.

"Can you imagine me thinking about marrying at my age?" she said pensively. "It's perfectly silly. Why, I should have my head examined. To think of leaving you and Biff now that you need me."

Mother went to the window and peered through the glass. "Here comes a car," she said. "My, we really are having a lot of company tonight."

"You might go so far as to say we are doing a helluva business," Gee Gee said.

I thought at first the car was for Joyce, then I heard a girlish giggling.

"Why, it's a little doll house," a woman's voice squealed.

"What fun to ride all the way to New York in a trailer," another voice said.

"Look how it hooks onto a car. Isn't that cute! But aren't you afraid to sit back when the car's moving?"

Then I heard Mandy.

"Afraid?" he said loudly. "Of course not. Not with good old Biffola driving. Now here's the front seat I was telling you about." He was beginning to sound like a landlord showing off an apartment to a prospective tenant. "You see, there's plenty of room for Millie up here. Now that Corny's not with us anymore I can double up with Biff on the army cot and Clarissima here can bunk with Gee Gee in the bedroom."

Biff went to the door and opened it slowly. Mandy pulled into the trailer with Millie and Clarissima.

"Look," he said, shoving the girls under Biff's nose. "I got us a couple new customers. We got it all figured out. We'll go sixes on the expenses. Millie can help with the driving too. They're both on their way east anyway, so I figured as long as we had the room I'd ask 'em to join us."

"Sure," Biff said. "Tickled to death to have you." The words were there but not the music. A tight smile was as far as he went in the personality department.

"I just ran into a guy that said he owned The Blinking Pup," Mandy was saying. "That guy had the nerve to tell me Dimples and Gee Gee were booked in his joint. I sure told him off. I told him no friends of mine would play a scratch house like that. He even let on like I might want to play it. Me? I'm no saloon actor. I know that now. I just wired the Gaiety and asked them if they could use a slightly used funny boy. That's for me. No more saloons for Mandy Hill!"

Gee Gee and Dimples were showing the girls around the trailer. Mandy followed, explaining the points of interest as they went along.

Mother had begun to wheeze again. Biff poured a small mound of asthma powder into the container lid and touched a match to it. When the flame died down, he reached for a towel and put it over Mother's head.

"Here's where we found the money," Mandy said. "Joyce is in the bedroom or I'd show you where we found the body." He had taken over Biff's job of Joe Host and he was working overtime at it.

"Soon as the inquest is over," he said, "we'll be rolling along. Back to the Gaiety with a quick one-two."

Mother's breathing became easier. She took the towel from

. head and folded it carefully over the back of her chair.

"My, oh my, that was a bad one," she said comfortably. Her smile was radiant, "You know, children," she said, "I've been thinking—"

Biff moaned softly.

"Hold your hats, boys," he said. "Here we go again."